MIDLIFE OR DEATH

Sweet Mountain Witches
Paranormal Women's Fiction Cozy Mystery
Book One

CINDY STARK

www.cindystark.com

Midlife or Death © 2021 C. Nielsen

ONE

Daisy?"

My best friend, Aeri Lambert, called to me, and I lifted a finger asking her to give me a moment. I finished filling a cup of coffee for the last in a steady stream of customers who'd come through my cat café, Meowkins Coffee, that morning. I appreciated the extra business considering that my small hometown was between busy seasons and that customers would drop to zero as soon as the street festival began that afternoon.

Sweet Mountain Meadows, the old mining town where I was born and raised, attracted a fair number of people who were looking to ski Utah in the winter or escape to the beautiful mountains in summer. But visitors waned once the snow began to melt and before the electric pink fireweed and vibrant orange Indian paintbrush on the mountain began to bloom.

I handed the coffee to my customer and turned to Aeri, who'd happily helped create cappuccinos and lattes with me nearly every morning for the past five years. We'd been friends since teenagers, but our relationship had deepened into something close to sisterhood once we began working together.

Though to look at us, we were nothing like sisters. She was a good six inches shorter than me, while I was tall. Most days, I wore my long blond hair woven into a loose braid, while Aeri kept her deep brown hair shorter. Where I was introverted, she always had a bright smile and bubbly personality that I envied.

Aeri motioned me toward the back counter where she scooped coffee beans into a grinder. When I was near enough, she spoke in a low voice that couldn't be heard by anyone sitting at the cozy walnut tables not far from us. "I've been thinking about the Beltane celebration tonight."

I released a heavy sigh. Not again. "Why bring that up on a perfectly good morning?"

Aeri shook her head in admonition, causing her straight, shiny hair to brush the tops of her shoulders. "You can't ignore this forever. Skip the street festival if you want, but this ritual is a momentous one, and the coven will expect you to be there."

And? "I don't know why I should care."

I really didn't. I'd stopped going to most of the coven's rituals ten years ago when I'd finally accepted that I'd never be like them. Practicing as a solitary witch brought me solace and peace.

"Because," Aeri insisted. "We'll learn who the replacement is for dearly-departed Fern, and you're in her line. It *could* be you."

I snorted and sent her an incredulous look. "We both know that's about as likely as Hades freezing over."

Aeri lifted a shoulder and let it drop. Hope for my future with the coven still sparked in my friend's eyes. "It could happen."

I dropped my chilly demeanor and gave her a kind smile. "Look, I appreciate you watching out for me, but truly, I'm happy with my life. I don't need to try to please people who don't care about me. But you should go, celebrate Beltane with the coven. Go with Brad to the street festival. You guys always have a good time, and you can tell me about everything later, okay?"

Aeri frowned in disappointment but nodded. I hoped, I really did, that this would be the last time she broached the subject. I didn't want to go, and that was that.

It took the appearance of one of my favorite customers to bring my mood back to good. I lifted a hand in greeting. "Hey, Gilbert. Your usual?"

Gilbert with his familiar gray whiskers and faded ballcap approached the counter. "You know it."

I glanced at him as I crafted his Americano. "How are you this fine morning?"

He patted his chest and then down his stomach with both hands. "Can't complain."

"Ellen?" I asked, lifting my brow. "Is she more relaxed now that the grandkids have headed home?"

Gilbert chuckled. "In some ways. But she's now got it in her head that I need to take her to the May Day thing tonight."

I nodded. Though the tradition of celebrating Beltane had resided solely within the coven for many, many years, at some point, it had expanded into the May Day event the whole town enjoyed.

I wasn't sure how many residents knew the extent of our gathering, though once midnight approached, we witches didn't hide as we donned our ritual robes and headed off into the woods carrying lanterns. But none of the townsfolk complained about the joviality and the abundance of handcrafted items and delicious food available for purchase at the festival.

Gilbert lifted his chin. "You'll be there, won't you? I know your mom always goes."

I shrugged. "Not sure."

Behind me, Aeri snorted. "Our Miss Daisy Summers doesn't want to go, Gilbert. I've tried talking her into it, but she's stubborn."

He caught my gaze and drew fuzzy gray brows together. "Why don't you want to go? It's supposed to be a lot of fun."

I narrowed my eyes into a friendly but accusatory gaze. "Hang on. Just a second ago, it sounded like you were complaining because your wife wanted you to go. Now, you're saying it's fun?"

Pink colored his cheeks. "That's because my joints will be stiff tomorrow from all the walking, but you're young. You should be out doing stuff."

I considered arguing that forty wasn't young and that my joints also ached when I overexerted. Instead, I smiled and handed the Americano coffee to him with a warm smile. "To each his own, I guess. Here you go, Gilbert. One Americano just like you like it."

He seemed grateful to be let off the hook. "You always make the best."

Gilbert lifted the cup to his lips as he turned away. A second later, he spat coffee all over my gray stone tiled floor. "What the..."

He cranked his head around to look at me with surprised disgust. "What did you do?"

I blinked in horror. "What do you mean? Is it bad?"

How could it be? The coffee beans were fresh, and I only used the finest mountain spring water.

He thrust the cup toward me. "See for yourself."

I pulled off the plastic lid and sniffed. Something akin to sulfur hit my nostrils, and I almost gagged. "Oh. That's terrible."

Gilbert agreed with a nod. "That's what I said."

Worry drew my brows together. "I'm so sorry. I just opened a new package of coffee beans and ground them myself this morning. They must be bad."

He frowned.

I lifted a hand to keep him from turning away. "If you can give me just a minute, I'll open a new bag and have a fresh Americano for you. Plus, I'll give you free coffee for the rest of the week."

His shoulders softened, and he smiled. "Okay, Miss Daisy. That sounds fair."

To sweeten the deal, I reached into the walnut and glass pastry case and plated his favorite treat, a blueberry muffin. "Here. You can munch on this while you wait."

He accepted her offering with a nod and headed toward the line of bar stools in front of the granite counter next to the big picture window. I loved that window, loved how it showcased the quaint streets of Sweet Mountain Meadows, which were now decorated with red, white, and green banners for Beltane.

I sighed and turned to Aeri with a confused expression. "I don't know what could have happened. No one else has complained about the espresso."

Aeri widened her eyes, looking perplexed. "I have no idea, but—"

She paused mid-sentence and narrowed her eyes. "Strike that. I think I know exactly what happened." She gestured with her head toward the front of the café.

I turned to see my biggest nemesis and her sister stroll through the front door, and everything suddenly made sense. My distant cousin Merry Mercer, with the family's coveted red hair and green eyes, had been a thorn in my side for decades. On the outside, she seemed to have the perfect life with her devoted husband and their lavish vacations.

She could put on a show and be fun and friendly...to everyone but me. People who didn't know her well loved her, and out of all the eligible witches I knew, I feared she would be the most likely to be chosen to take Fern's place and serve on the council.

Her sister Oriana Nixon wasn't as blatantly contemptuous, but she had no problem following in her sister's rude and crude footsteps most of the time. Maybe being like me and not blessed with the Summers' red hair had humbled Oriana enough to make her tolerable on her good days.

Though I would have happily traded my blond hair for her chestnut strands with a fair amount of red, even if they did always look a bit windblown. I sometimes wondered if Oriana felt she had to act like her bully of a sister or risk becoming her next victim.

Aeri spoke beneath her breath. "I'll get Gilbert's Americano while you deal with that lot."

Merry approached the counter and stared down her nose into the glass pastry display. Her leather jacket was open, revealing a green silk blouse that accentuated her eyes and displayed an ample amount of cleavage.

Oriana trailed behind, looking like a watered-down version of her sister in a faded hunter green sweater and jeans. She slipped a sideways glance toward Gilbert, erasing the last bit of doubt in my mind about who'd ruined his coffee.

I steeled my nerves in preparation for the encounter with my cousins. Though I was much less vulnerable to Merry's cruel taunts than I had been in my youth, she still had a way of getting under my skin. "Hello, Merry. What brings you to my humble coffee shop today?"

My cousin met my gaze and twisted her lips into what she probably thought was a smile. "Oh, you know. Oriana and I have been out shopping. I decided I needed a new pair of shoes for tonight. Unfortunately, the line of people at our favorite coffee shop was super long, and we thought why not support your café? After all, family is family."

I held back a snort. Merry had never treated me with anything more than disdain, and I was certain she'd go back to her favorite shop the next time she was out. I smiled anyway. "Wonderful. What can I get for you?"

Merry released a long sigh and turned her gaze to the blackboard over my head. "Just a plain coffee. I can be a bit of a snob when it comes to how I like my chai tea."

Oriana met my gaze and held it. I sensed anger pulsing from her, but I couldn't fathom why. Unless she'd lost her patience with Merry.

"Same for me," Oriana said as she continued to stare.

As if she'd dare to order anything different or stand up to Merry. Really, the way she let her sister push her around was sad. I rang up their coffees, focused on Merry, and gave her the total cost for their drinks.

Merry lifted her brow. "What? No family discount?"

I knew for a fact that Merry's husband made good money, and she wanted a discount for coffees that were only a couple of bucks each? "Oh, sorry. If finances are tight, I'd be happy to comp one for each of you."

Merry straightened her spine. "Of course, I can afford it. In fact, Bill received another promotion last week. Next thing you know, he'll be running the company."

I should have felt guilty for pushing her buttons, but she made it so hard to be nice. I widened my eyes as though I was happy for her. "That's great. Are you paying for Oriana's coffee, too?"

Maybe that would settle Oriana's irritation.

Merry blinked several times, and I was certain she was trying to figure a way out of paying for both.

Oriana held up a hand. "I can pay for my own."

Merry shushed her with a wave. "Of course, I'll treat Oriana to coffee. It's the least I can do for what she's endured."

I was curious to know what Oriana had experienced, but I tried to mind my own business. If Oriana wanted me to know, she'd tell me. Though I couldn't help but wonder if perhaps she was having marital trouble. Her husband could be an immature oaf sometimes. Plus, that might explain her mood.

Instead of commenting, I happily took Merry's credit card and swiped it.

I handed the card back to her just as a man with a mysterious air about him strolled through the café's door. He was taller than me, with dark hair that had been shaved close above his ears but grew longer on top, giving him a rugged, tousled look. If his stance was any indication, he exuded self-confidence.

For the briefest of moments, his gaze met mine, and he dipped his head in greeting.

I offered a small smile and refocused on my cousins. "It will be just a few minutes, if you want to wait by the bar stools."

I lifted my chin and gazed over Oriana's head at Mr. Dark and Mysterious to indicate that they needed to move along. "I can help you if you're ready."

Merry and Oriana glanced behind them, and immediately, an interested smile curved Merry's lips. She was married, but that had never been the slightest deterrent to her where beautiful men were concerned. I felt a twinge of sympathy for her husband Carl, wherever he might be, unaware of what a flirt his wife was when they were apart.

The stranger shook his head. "It's fine. Go ahead and chat. I'm still trying to decide."

Just my luck.

A sly smile lifted the corners of Merry's lips as she turned back to me. "You haven't forgotten about the ritual tonight, have you? I wouldn't want you to miss it like you have the past several years."

And there it was. I'd known from the moment my cousins had walked in that the conversation would eventually lead in that direction. Merry assumed she'd be chosen, and she wanted as many people as possible to witness her triumph. "No worries. I haven't forgotten."

Merry continued as though I hadn't spoken. "The celebration is a special one this year, you know. They'll be picking a replacement for Fern."

The stranger shifted his gaze from the blackboard to Merry, seeming interested in the topic of their conversation. I couldn't exactly blame him for eavesdropping since the café was quiet enough now that he could overhear.

He caught me watching him and lifted his gaze back to the menu.

Arie brought the two cups of coffee to the counter, and I fitted a lid on the first one. "Yes, we're all so excited to see who will be chosen."

Oriana slid a glance toward her sister, and I wondered if she secretly hoped that it might be her.

I hoped it would be neither. "I'm sure Katelyn will be there. I've always found her to be a quietly confident woman with knowhow and a forthright manner."

Merry looked at me as if I'd lost my mind. "Katelyn? Do you really believe she has what it takes to lead?"

I shrugged. "As much as anyone."

Oriana shook her head. "Being such an outcast, you're hardly qualified to judge."

The anger coming from Oriana was palpable, and I wished I knew why. I fitted the lid on the second cup of coffee and slid them forward on the counter. Hopefully, they'd take them and leave. "Here you go. I hope you have a wonderful morning."

Unfortunately, neither of them moved.

Merry narrowed her eyes. "Will you be bringing a date, then?"

Heat generated by embarrassment raced to my cheeks, more so because of the mysterious man, who I was sure was still listening.

I should have known it would be a mistake to mention Katelyn and stir the monster inside Merry because I knew how ruthless she could be. She'd fight to the death if she felt someone had gotten one up on her. So, of course, she'd bring up the lack of men in my life.

She was correct that I'd never dated much. Because I was unfortunate enough to have been born into what some in the coven called "a dead line", I'd been overlooked as a viable marriage candidate by the men in town from witch families, too. Sure, I could have dated and perhaps married someone without a magical bloodline, but those relationships were always messy at best. "I guess you'll have to wait and see."

It was the best I could do to save face.

Merry gave me a smug smile. "I guess we will."

She snatched her cup of coffee and headed toward the door. Oriana, however, remained. She stared at me with a harsh gaze. "I'd like my ring back."

I blinked in surprise. "Your ring?"

Her anger spilled across the counter and ran toward me. "*Yes.* The family heirloom."

I vaguely recalled that she'd inherited a ruby ring from a long-ago grandmother in our line, but I had no idea why she thought I would have it. I shook my head. "I don't have your ring, Oriana. There's no reason I would."

She narrowed her gaze. "Unless you stole it."

Merry realized Oriana hadn't followed her, and she returned to the counter greatly annoyed. She gripped her sister's arm. "Come on," Merry said once again.

Oriana turned to Merry, her jaw set with a stubbornness that I hadn't seen in her before. "I want my ring back."

"Don't worry. We'll get it back," Merry said and pulled her away from the counter.

Oriana hesitated and ultimately gave in to her sister. She pointed a sharp finger at me. *"This isn't over."*

I closed my eyes for a few seconds, searching for a bit of solace or understanding about what had just taken place. When none came, I let a stressed breath fizzle out of me.

Then I opened my eyes, focused on the man, and smiled.

TWO

The intriguing stranger stepped up to the counter, and I met his gaze, doing my best to pretend the entire embarrassing incident with my cousins hadn't happened. "Good morning. Welcome to Meowkins Coffee. What can I get for you?"

He smiled then, a smile so perfect that it charmed me completely. "Hello, my lovely. I would like to try your Cat-puccino, I think. Is it good?"

I nodded, feeling like a robot. "Yes, of course."

I probably should have given him the spiel about how the espresso comes from the finest coffee beans, et cetera, but something about him had thrown my senses off track. Or perhaps the residue from my annoying cousins was still messing with me.

His smile grew bigger, and I wondered if he knew how his height, the carefree style of his dark hair, and those engaging green eyes affected the ladies. "I'll take a large, then," he said and held a credit card toward me.

Good thing I wasn't easily swayed, and I regained my better senses quickly. I took his card, rang up the sale, and then pointed toward the row of bar stools lined against the counter that looked out onto the street.

"If you want to wait over there, we'll call your name when it's ready."

He arched his brow. "But you didn't ask my name."

It was my turn to smile at him. I briefly glanced at the credit card before handing it back to him. "Gideon McKay."

He dipped his head and took the card. "Well played."

He said it as though we were engaged in a game of chess, which I'll admit did intrigue me. I watched as he strolled to the bar stools and hitched half his butt on the seat. Instead of pulling out his phone like most customers did while they waited, he settled his gaze on me once again, leaving me flustered. I immediately immersed myself in my job and pulled a shot of espresso into his cup.

Since he'd arrived in town between our two best seasons, I guessed he was likely there on business. That thought led me to wonder if he had anything to do with the proposed new resort on the outskirts of town. If so, he might not get the friendliest reception from many of the residents who liked Sweet Mountain Meadows just the way it was.

The man seemed quite comfortable in his ivory cable-knit sweater though the temperature was warming up outside. The sweater paired well with his gray slacks, giving him a fashionable look. Unfortunately, he looked maybe thirty, which put him at least ten years younger than me.

Not that I was interested. Though it would be funny to show up at the festival with him and see the look on Merry's face.

But, no. I'd had enough drama for the day. My idea of a good time was serving great coffee and helping to save rescue kitties. They brought me plenty of love and company, not to mention a great deal of satisfaction when they found their forever homes.

People like to mock crazy cat ladies, but it was a fulfilling way of life, which was why there were enough of us in the world for someone to coin that term in the first place.

Still, that didn't mean I couldn't appreciate a nice-looking man when he walked into my coffee shop.

Aeri nudged me with her elbow. "Oh, my," she whispered.

"Umm-hmm," I said beneath my breath, agreeing with her assessment.

Not that Aeri was looking for a man, either. She'd been married to her high school sweetheart for twenty-three years, and I didn't expect that to change.

Playing along with her silliness, I fluttered my eyes in a flirtatious way.

And then he cleared his throat.

I slowly shifted my gaze toward the handsome man and found him staring straight at me. I feared he'd caught me and my embarrassing expression, but there was no way he could have overheard us.

I hoped.

Aeri deserted me and busied herself cleaning up the back counter while I steamed milk, but I could sense her interest in him as well. Normally, I could read people within a few seconds of meeting them, but this guy was different. I wondered if Aeri had thought the same.

Unfortunately, I couldn't put my finger on what made him unique.

I'd just added the foam to his cappuccino in my signature paw-print design, when I caught a flash of gray fur out the corner of my eye. By the time I'd fully wrenched my gaze around, my cat Freya had raced across the floor and jumped onto the counter in front of Gideon. "No," I said, dragging out the word.

Cats were not allowed in the section where I served food. I could lose my license if a health inspector walked in.

I abandoned Gideon's drink and rushed around the counter, snatching my fluffy gray cat from the granite. "What are you doing?" I said, gazing into her perceptive green eyes. "You know you can't be out here."

Most people would think I was silly to admonish a cat in such a way, but she truly did understand me when I spoke to her, and she darned well knew that she was not allowed in the front of the coffee shop. Besides violating all kinds of health codes, some customers were allergic to cats, and I wanted my shop to be a place where everyone felt welcome.

She meowed at me and struggled to get free.

I gave her a look, asking what had gotten into her.

"It's okay," Gideon said. "I like cats. It's one of the reasons I chose your shop. Though I thought a cat café would have more than one kitty on site."

I exhaled my relief, grateful to hear that Freya's appearance hadn't bothered him. The last thing I needed was a fussy customer when my familiar was being unruly.

I thumbed over my shoulder to show Gideon the general direction of the door leading to the back area where my current furry friends hung out until they found their forever homes. "Actually, we do have more cats, but they're housed in the Purry Parlor, which is where this little lady should be. I'm required to keep the two areas separate, but customers can take their purchases into the parlor if they like."

He lifted his brow. "Purry Parlor? Sounds like my kind of place."

A mysterious man who liked cats? Intriguing, indeed. "Are you interested in adding an hour of cat visitation to your purchase? We charge a small fee to help pay for the costs of housing the cats until they're adopted. Except Freya, of course. She's mine."

He studied Freya and then nodded. "As a matter of fact, it does sound like a lovely way to pass an hour or so."

He stood, pulled out his wallet, and set his credit card on the counter. "I'll trade you this for your cat."

Typically, Freya didn't like others to hold her, but when he held out his hands, she struggled to be free again. Not knowing what else to do, I let him take her, and she shifted to look at his face.

He stroked the top of her head and then scratched her chin. "You are a very beautiful lady."

Her purrs echoed loudly, and I widened my eyes. Apparently, my cat also appreciated a charming man.

I swiped his credit card from the counter and placed a hand on his elbow, urging him forward. "Come this way."

I pulled open the glass door that would allow him entrance into my cat sanctuary that currently housed nine cats looking to be adopted. Nicole Santoro, who managed the parlor for me, widened her eyes in surprise. She placed Angel, the white kitty she'd been brushing, onto the floor and hurried toward us.

Nicole briefly glanced at Gideon, her eyes showing interest, before she directed her gaze to me. "Oh, Daisy. I'm so sorry. I don't know how Freya managed to escape. You know I keep a close eye on all the cats."

That she did, but my little minx could be sneaky when she wanted. "It's okay," I said. "I'll wash up and put on a new apron. No worries. Plus, Mr. McKay here should keep her occupied for a while."

Gideon smiled at Nicole, who brightened immediately. He did have that effect on people. And cats.

"Oh," Nicole said. "Freya's already made a friend. Nice. It's been quiet back here this morning, and I'm sure all the cats will be happy to look at someone besides me."

He lifted his brow. "I should think they would enjoy the company of a lovely lady."

Nicole blushed, and I chuckled to myself. Out of my two friends and me, Nicole *was* the one who might be interested in Mr. Mysterious.

I reached out and scratched Freya's head before I lifted my gaze to Gideon. "I'll be right back with your cappuccino."

Questions about the new man in town tumbled through my head as I made him a fresh cup and headed back to the parlor with it and his credit card. Nicole met me at the door and took the items. A bright pink blush still hovered on her cheeks, and I grinned. "Hmm?" I asked, knowing she'd understand my question.

She quickly shook her head. "You know I'm with Cliff."

I shrugged because we both knew Cliff was a loser, but Nicole turned away, cutting off any further discussion on her choice of men.

I hesitated in the doorway long enough to watch Nicole stroll to Gideon with his coffee. He sat in an overstuffed chair that he'd semi reclined, with Freya laying square on his chest, and he looked like the most relaxed man in the world.

Not that I was surprised. Cats did have a way of calming the soul.

I might have stuck around longer to see if I could sense a spark of attraction between the two, but I had work to do.

THREE

When Gideon and Nicole emerged from the Purry Parlor, I glanced at the clock on the screen in front of me. He'd stayed well past the hour he'd paid for, but I wasn't about to mention it. The cats loved the company, and I loved them.

Gideon stopped just beyond the doors to the Parlor and turned to Nicole. I couldn't hear what he said to her, but it brought a smile to her face. Maybe Nicole was more interested than she'd let on. Or perhaps Gideon had charmed his way into her heart. I suspected a man like him could do that.

On his way out the door, he paused and waited until I'd fully focused on him. He gave a small bow and then smiled. "You have a most delightful place here, Daisy. Thank you for sharing it with me."

His kind words and charming manner warmed my cheeks. I nodded in appreciation. "Thank you. I hope you'll come back and see us."

He lifted his brow in a way that melted my heart a little. "You may count on it."

With that, he exited the café, leaving a cloud of interesting energy in his wake. Nicole joined me at the counter, though she watched him out the big picture window. "Vampire?" she mused.

I studied him as he walked away, and I shook my head. "I don't think so. Too much color to his skin."

Aeri's arm brushed mine as she found a spot next to me and sighed. "Imagine if all our customers were that delightful."

I chuckled. "Not just our customers. What if everyone was that kind?"

"And handsome," Nicole added.

With Gideon now out of sight, I shifted my gaze to Nicole. "I think he likes you. He stayed back there with you for well past an hour."

She snorted and pinned me with a look. "He talked about you the entire time, Daisy. He wanted to know how long you've lived here. How long you've had your café. He also sensed that Freya was a special kind of pet and had a unique connection to you."

Her words surprised me, and I'll admit made me a little nervous. "Why was he so curious about me? That seems a little creepy, doesn't it?"

Didn't it? Why me, of all people? "I hope you didn't tell him much," I said.

Nicole shrugged off my concerns. "It didn't come off as creepy at all. I think he might be smitten."

"No," I said with a small snort of denial. "I'm certain that's not the case. If it wasn't you, then it must be the cats."

Aeri grinned. "I think he likes you, too, Daisy. Didn't you see the way he watched you when he was out here?"

Yeah, I'd caught him staring. "My point exactly. His gaze was unnerving."

Nicole and Aeri shared a look. "Our point exactly," Nicole said. "His attraction unnerved you."

I scoffed. "I don't think so. I've been around the block a few times, and I know when a man is attracted to me."

Though that might have been a bit of an exaggeration.

Nicole started to argue, but I held up a hand. "You two can discuss this all you want. I'm headed out for a few hours. I told my mom that I'd bring her lunch."

The expressions on both their faces turned to worry. Aeri placed a comforting hand on my shoulder. "How is she doing? Any better?"

I gave a small nod. "A little, actually. Her doctor told her yesterday that she should be able to walk without assistance in another three weeks. Of course, she'll have rehab for a while."

Nicole flashed the warm and generous smile that she was known for. "That's great news.

Aeri agreed, and I thanked them both for their concern. Then I grabbed my purse from the backroom, and when I emerged, I caught my two friends still talking about Gideon. I shook my head at their ridiculousness and headed out into the fresh late-spring air that was fragrant with the scent of pine, lilacs, and hummed with the energy of new life.

After stopping to pick up lunch, I found my mom at the back of her small house sitting in her favorite chair. Morning sunshine filtered through her big windows and provided a perfect view of the surrounding mountains, including the waterfall that cascaded from the tops of the rocks in the distance. "Hey, Mum."

I walked forward and kissed her on the cheek. My mom had never married, which was likely my future as well. Bridget Summers kept her gray hair short now, though she'd had it long most of her life. Very few wrinkles lined her beautiful face, but a lifetime of hardship and worry still dimmed her features.

She closed the romance novel she'd been reading and set it on the small cherrywood table next to her chair. That table had been passed down through generations of Summers women, and I was proud to know that someday it would be mine.

Although I wasn't sure where it would go after me since I didn't intend to have children. Maybe to Katelyn, the one distant cousin I still claimed. I think our great grandmothers had been sisters. Katelyn *was* in thick with the coven, but she'd never treated me any differently. I respected her for that.

"Hello, Daisy, dear," my mom said.

I eyed her book and lifted a teasing brow. "Still reading those spicy romance novels, I see."

She chuckled and then waved away my comment. "There's nothing wrong with believing in true love."

"Except that it doesn't happen in real life. You and I are perfect examples."

She lifted her chin in defiance. "I'll have you know that I loved your father, and he loved me."

I widened my eyes in surprise and wondered if her pain medication had affected her more than she realized. "You've never talked about my father like that before. You've always made it seem as if he'd deserted you once you found out you were pregnant with me."

She gave a small grunt of dismissal. "Sometimes people don't talk about the past because it pains them too much."

If that was true, then thoughts of my father must cause her a great deal of distress because she rarely brought him up. I wished she'd tell me more, but her statement made it clear that what she'd said to me about their relationship was all she intended to disclose today.

But it was a start. If the pain in her heart had lessened enough for her to tell me that much, maybe more was to come. I hoped so. I knew he'd been her lover and that the details of her history were hers to share if and when she wanted. But he was also my father, and I hated that she'd left him a blank slate for most of my life.

I didn't know how to respond except for my usual answer. "I'm sorry that he hurt you."

She lifted her green eyes to me. "My only regret is that his absence has left you so cynical about love. One day, you'll see."

I withheld my eye roll and changed the subject to lunch. "Would you like to eat in here or the kitchen?"

Her expression switched to one of delight. "What did you bring me?"

I smiled, grateful that I could bring her some happiness. "Only your favorite. Linguini and vegetables from Deliziosa."

She placed both hands over her stomach. "Wonderful. I'm starving. Let's eat in here."

I headed to the kitchen where I transferred our food to plates and placed them on a tray along with ice water and napkins.

By the time I returned, my mom had made space on the coffee table so that we had room to eat.

We ate in companionable silence, and I took a moment to savor how well the lightly steamed carrots and broccoli tasted when mixed with the alfredo sauce from my linguini. I loved this dish every bit as much as my mom did.

When she finished her last bite, she wiped her mouth, which removed most of the pink lipstick she insisted on wearing even though she wouldn't leave the house. She placed the napkin on her empty plate. "I'm glad you came today, Daisy. There's something I've been meaning to talk to you about."

That sentence was never followed by anything good, and my contentment evaporated into a thin mist that floated away. "What's that?" I said, still trying to keep the mood light.

My mom drew her brows together, deepening the worry wrinkles on her forehead. "When Aeri stopped by the other day, she told me that you're not going to the Beltane celebration. Why not?"

I sent her a look that questioned her sanity. "Why would I? You know I don't fit in with them, and I haven't gone to anything official for ages."

She waved away my excuse. "You've never given them a chance."

Uh...I was pretty sure that I had. Plenty of them. "Really, Mum, it doesn't matter if I go or not. So, let's talk about something else."

I sensed her stubborn streak emerging and wished I could will it away. "It matters to me, Daisy. With Fern's passing, someone from our line will be chosen. I can't go to represent our family, so I need you to be there."

Though I didn't intend to vocalize my internal groan, it came out anyway. "Mum, you know our leg of the line will die with me. There's no way I'll be chosen. Besides, the coven has never treated you all that well, either. Why do you hang onto a hope that's as dead as poor Fern?"

My mom blinked rapidly, and I realized I'd made her cry. Which made me the worst daughter ever. Especially when she'd been so down lately, not to mention she'd had some serious complications during her knee replacement that had made me wonder if I'd become an orphan sooner than later.

I sighed, set my plate on the coffee table in front of us, and turned more fully toward her. "I'm sorry. I didn't mean to upset you. I just don't want to be around them."

She pulled a wrinkled tissue from her bra and dabbed at her eyes. "I know, Daisy, dear. I shouldn't have asked. Just because it's *so* important to me, doesn't mean it is to you."

Ugh. Mothers and their guilt trips.

I remained quiet, hoping that she'd let the moment pass, but instead, she lifted her gaze, wet lashes and all, and focused on me with hope shimmering in her eyes.

I snorted. "The celebration is tonight, Mum. You know I burned my old ritual robe years ago. I have nothing, and I mean nothing, to wear. Would you like me to go naked?"

In many years past, that's exactly how the witches had celebrated, but times had changed except for personal, small party gatherings. Thank heavens because I really didn't want to see everyone that I knew naked.

I exhaled my frustration. When she didn't immediately respond, I figured the argument was over. As much as my mother would like me to attend, she wouldn't dream of sending me in her place not dressed for the occasion.

But then I caught sight of a smile blossoming on her face and triumph twinkled in her irises. "That's not a problem at all, dear. Ever since talking to Aeri, I've been thinking of solutions, and I have the perfect one."

Aeri. She was supposed to be *my* best friend, which meant she shouldn't be siding with my mother.

For now, I indulged my mom. I widened my eyes with interest and pretended that she had a chance to convince me. Then at least she could feel like she'd tried her best. "And what would that be?" I asked.

She shifted and pointed at the ornate wooden trunk that had huddled in a dark corner of my mother's sitting room for as long as I could remember. As a child, I'd sit and trace the flowers and swirls made from little brass studs that decorated the edges, and I'd imagine what magical things might be in it.

As a teenager, I'd tried to open it many times, but my powers couldn't overcome whatever spell she'd used to keep the contents private. I'd asked my mom many times what she kept inside, but she'd always responded by saying that someday she'd tell me.

"Be a dear, and drag that old chest over here to me, please," she said.

FOUR

My long dormant curiosity surged as I wrapped my fingers around the iron handles on the sides of the old leather and wood chest and lifted.

Or not.

The strain pulled a muscle in my lower back, and I groaned in response. I immediately straightened as though that would undo the damage. Unfortunately, it didn't, and I knew I'd be feeling it for days.

Whatever my mom had stored inside weighed a ton.

She clucked her disapproval. "Bless the stars, girl. You're going to break your back if you try to lift it yourself. Use your magic for the Goddess's sake."

Annoyed because I hadn't been a girl for a long time and I shouldn't have needed her to remind me, I shifted a narrow-eyed gaze in her direction. "Now you tell me."

She snorted. "I thought you had enough sense to use your magic without me telling you to."

I rolled my eyes instead of responding and turned back to the old chest. I whispered the spell that would briefly disable gravity, and the chest rose several inches above the worn gray carpet. I took hold of an iron handle once again. This time, the chest followed along with me quite nicely with only a little effort needed to guide its direction.

When I was close to my mother's chair, I released the spell, and it landed on the carpet with a plunk.

"Oh," my mom said and gasped. "Careful dear. It's very old."

I murmured an apology, knowing that I'd dropped it a little harder than I should have, as though punishing it for the dull ache in my lower back would help me feel better.

My mom scooted to the edge of her chair and leaned forward. She held out a hand, and the chest inched closer to her. Her hand shook mildly as she placed it on top of the old wooden box and held it there for a moment. Then, she lifted the lid.

A sly grin played on her lips when she glanced up at me. "It will only open for me. After my death, that power will transfer to you."

I didn't want to talk about the day she might leave me, but I did lift my chin in acknowledgement so that she didn't bother repeating herself.

The box sat between us, and the lid, when opened, partially blocked my view of the contents. I shifted my stance, trying to get a better look at what was hidden inside.

An exhale filled with wonder escaped my mom's lips as she gazed into the box. She reached inside and pulled out a bundle that had been wrapped in tissue. Hints of something made from ivory-colored cloth peeked through tears in the thin paper. She set it on her lap and carefully removed the layers of tissue to reveal a cloak with ornate gold and white taffeta trim.

My mom drew her fingers across the soft-looking fabric with a reverence that the beautiful piece of clothing deserved. She didn't need to tell me it was special. "Aibreann's ritual robe," she said quietly.

I widened my eyes in surprise. "Aibreann? As in my grandmother who lived hundreds of years ago?"

Bridget lifted her gaze to me and nodded.

I couldn't believe such a valued treasure had been living in the house with me the whole time while I'd been growing up. I inhaled a slow, anticipatory breath. *"Where did you get it?"*

She smiled. "From my mother and her mother before her, and so on."

I knelt on the floor near my mom's feet, which wasn't as easy as it had been when I was twenty. The magnetic energy from the soft-looking cloak reached toward me before I touched it. With one finger, I traced the stitching along the edge of the hood. "This is incredible."

I knew I sounded dumbfounded, but I couldn't help it. People didn't pull things like this out of closets or chests anymore. Most items from that era had been lost during the passing of time or resided in a museum somewhere.

I met her gaze, and she watched me with a look of pure happiness. "My mother told me to save it for a special day. The time never seemed right for me to wear it, but my heart tells me it's right for you."

Her comment knocked me off my haunches, and I landed on my butt on the carpet behind me. I shook my head, slowly at first and then faster. "No. There's no way I could possibly wear this. What if I ruined it? Spilled mead on it or something?"

My mom's laughter was like sunshine dancing on crystals. Light and pretty. "Don't worry. It's protected from such things. How do you think it's managed to stay beautiful for so long?"

I shook my head, still not quite comprehending what was in front of me. "I...don't know. Magic, I guess."

She snorted. "Of course, it's magic. Here, hold it up. Better yet, try it on."

I wanted to wrap such a magnificent piece of clothing around me. I truly did, but something held me back. Something in my heart that told me this moment was more monumental than it appeared. My breath escaped in a slow exhale. "I..."

My mother narrowed her gaze in disappointment. "Daisy Mae Summers. You will try this on right now."

I swallowed, her tone making me feel like fourteen again instead of forty. I got to my feet and gently took the cloak from her. I undid the gold metal clasp that held it together and carefully slid the lovely garment across my shoulders before I fastened it once again around my neck.

Powerful energy sparked and snapped where it touched me, and then it felt as though it had wrapped me in a warm hug. It was as if my great-grandmother's love had traveled through the centuries to me. The next thing I knew, I was blinking back tears. I had no idea where they'd come from, but there they were, expressing my emotions where words would have never sufficed.

My mom tucked her hands beneath her chin. "Bless the stars, Daisy. You are glowing."

I lifted fingertips to my cheek and sensed the wild energy surging there. "It's beyond amazing. It's exquisite. You should try it on."

Bridget shook her head. "No. I never have. It never felt right, and now I know why. I believe Aibreann intended this for you. For this night. I feel that to the deepest depth of my core."

I wanted to argue with her, but I sensed something truly magical was at play. "How could she know about me when I wouldn't be born for hundreds of years?"

My mother shrugged. "I don't know, but she did." She inhaled a quick breath that caught my attention. "Daisy, Aibreann wore this on the night she was chosen to serve with the high council. I believe the same might happen with you."

Uh, no. Now, she was taking things a little too far. I wouldn't argue with her and douse her pleasure, though. Time could do that for her. Regardless, it appeared I was going to the celebration after all. I couldn't turn her down after such a gift.

"Oh, crap," I said as the reality of getting ready for the event dropped like stones, creating a mountain in front of me. "I have no dress to wear with this. Those strappy silver sandals I bought years ago would work, but..."

My mom lifted a finger and grinned. "Never fear, darling. I've got your back."

Except, she'd never used that phrase in her life, which only deepened my worries.

She dug deep into her chest, shifting several items, one of which looked like an ancient tome, and she produced another tissue wrapped package. This time, she wasn't as careful when she opened it. "My mother bought me this for Beltane the year I turned twenty-one."

I opened my mouth to insist I could find something else, mostly because I was certain her style would never match mine. But I lost my words at the sight of a limp, chiffon dress in colors that I imagined must have been a delicate spring green and the soft lavender of lilacs at one time.

"Oh, no," my mom whispered, and I could feel her heart breaking.

"Oh, no," I echoed, wanting to help her feel better, but not super disappointed that her dress was unwearable. "It looks as though it must have been beautiful."

Bridget tore the rest of the tissue away from the diaphanous fabric and tossed it aside. She turned the dress this way and that, clucking as she did. "This won't do. It just won't do."

I lifted my shoulders in a disappointed shrug. "It's okay. I'll ask Aeri or Nicole. One of them must have something that I can borrow."

My mother's features twisted into a stern expression. "No, I mean it simply will not do to leave the dress in this state. Put it on for me so I can see what I'm doing."

What she was...doing?

Once again, I wanted to object. Hadn't I indulged her enough for one afternoon?

She lifted expectant brows, and I knew I couldn't deny the woman who'd had so little joy in her life. "Okay. I'll do it, but then I must get back to the café. I can check with Aeri and Nicole about something to wear once I get there."

She handed the dress to me and then twirled her fingers, encouraging me to hurry. Which wasn't a bad idea. The sooner I tried on the dress, the sooner I could take it off and be on my way.

The zipper in back protested as I drew it downward, reminding me of a little old lady who'd been sitting in her rocking chair for too long. I slipped off my pale pink Meowkins t-shirt and tossed it aside and then gathered the skirt to lift it over my head.

I did like the feel of the filmy fabric, the way it whispered against my skin as it slipped down my torso. But there was no way it could be repaired. Time had wreaked its damage as it did with all things. Unless they had been magically protected like the cloak.

Once I had my mother's dress over my head, I pulled the bodice forward and slid the ribbon straps over and up my arms. I turned so my mother could zip it.

She got the zipper as far as my mid back, but we both knew neither of us was the size we were in our twenties. The dress accommodated my wider hips because the skirt was full and flowy, but that was about it. "It's not going to fit, Mum. Maybe if I had six months to drop some weight, but not today."

"Oh, hush," my mom said impatiently.

She reached into her old chest and pulled out a gnarled wand that had been sanded and stained to give it a rich umber color. I widened my eyes in surprise. "You're going to use a wand?"

Who even did that anymore? Witches had known for a century that wands were only a tool to direct power and that a finger would work just as well.

My mom's eyes sparked with fire. "There are powers in the old ways. Never forget that."

I could give her a list of formidable witches who would argue against the need for wands, but if it made her feel more powerful to use it, then that's exactly what it would be.

She moved behind me and began to whisper. I tried to look over my shoulder to see what she was doing, but I only caught glimpses of her swaying as she used the wand to direct her magic.

Then the tightness around my ribcage eased, and I glanced downward. The faded colors of the diaphanous dress grew brighter, and it was literally as though my mom was breathing new life into it. The wrinkled and crushed fabric seemed to ease and smooth, and the next thing I knew, I was immersed in a timeless dress more beautiful than I could have imagined.

A quiet gasp escaped my lips. "Oh, Mum. This is so pretty. When did you learn how to fix clothing? You're not a sewing witch."

My mom finished zipping the dress and then moved until she faced me. She looked me up and down and then grinned. "I still have the touch."

"The touch?" I asked, amazed at her work.

"Yes," she said as a blush colored her cheeks. "I actually enjoyed creating garments in my younger days. I'd thought I might have become a designer when I grew up."

I smoothed the petal-shaped strips of pale green and lavender that made up the overskirt. "Why didn't you?"

My mom waved her hand at my question as though that would diminish it. "Oh, you know. I fell in love and then you came along. I had more important things to think about."

The idea that my existence might have killed her dreams didn't sit well with me. But perhaps there was still time for her to explore her passion. "Maybe you'd like to start again?"

She gave me a placating smile. "Stop worrying about me. You need to get going. You have a special celebration to attend, and you'll need to have time to spend at the hair salon."

I frowned and drew a hand over my hair that I'd pulled back into a haphazard bun. I supposed freshening my color and covering the gray strands that had snuck up on me would match my outfit better. "Yes, okay. I need to go."

My mom unzipped me and folded the cloak while I slipped out of the dress. Then she gently smoothed my dress that I'd handed to her and carefully returned it and the cloak back to me. "I truly wish I could be there tonight, dear Daisy. Have Aeri send me a picture of you all once you're together, okay?"

Unexpected emotion welled behind my eyes, and I blinked. "Of course."

She lifted a shoulder and let it drop. "If you are chosen, you'll be sure to call, right? I don't want to be the last to know."

I snorted but smiled. "Yes, Mom. If such a crazy thing happens, I'll call you."

Then I was back outside in the bright sunshine, feeling like my life had changed drastically during the time from when I'd entered my mom's house to when I'd left.

It hadn't, really. Other than I'd learned more about my mom, including the fact that she had some unbelievable things in that old chest and that whatever else was in there would one day be mine.

FIVE

That evening, I waited just inside my front door, watching for Nicole to arrive to pick me up. I patted the pockets of the cloak for the fifth time to ensure that I'd remembered the magical items I'd need for the ceremony later.

The nervous flutters that had started the moment I put on my mother's dress had increased in strength as minutes ticked by. I was going with Nicole to the celebration, since Cliff refused to accompany her. Part of me didn't blame him because I didn't want to be there, either. But he never supported Nicole in anything, so I still reserved the right to call him a loser.

Nicole's older silver sedan slid into my driveway, and I turned to Freya who watched me with amusement. I exhaled a deep breath and stared into her perceptive green eyes. "I wish I could take you with me."

She meowed in response and dipped her head in a nod.

Familiars had been allowed once upon a time, but someone's fox had caught someone's bird, causing an uproar, and witches had fired spells left and right, some of which had knocked down trees. The scars on their trunks could still be seen today. After that, it had been decided that familiars should be left at home.

I gave Freya one last smile before I walked out the door. "Wish me luck."

Cool spring air chilled my heated cheeks and refreshed my soul. I carried the ritual cloak over my arm because my nerves had made it too stifling to wear, but I'd be grateful for it later when the coven held their official ceremony in the woods.

The silky fabric of the dress swished against my bare legs as I walked toward the car. Nicole climbed from the driver's seat and strolled toward me to give me a hug. "Oh, my Goddess, Daisy. You are stunning. You must have washed your face with the morning dew."

I had, because I wasn't about to ignore a tradition as old as time that might make me look younger, but I wasn't going to admit it. I held up a hand. "Stop. You're only making this worse."

She gave a light snort. "Sorry. I know you're more comfortable in jeans and a t-shirt, but bless the stars, that look suits you."

"Thanks. Crazily enough, my mom had been storing this dress and my cloak for years."

Nicole grinned. "They're gorgeous. You're gorgeous."

I snorted. "If you want to talk stunning, look in the mirror, Nicole Santoro."

Her ornate ivory ritual cloak covered most of her dress, but the soft pink of her flowing skirt set off her dark curls, and she smiled. I pointed toward her plunging neckline. "Cliff is insane to let you walk out of the house like that. Some guy is going to snatch you away from him, and he'll be crying the rest of his life. Maybe that Gideon guy will show tonight."

Nicole rolled her eyes and headed for the car. "Cliff doesn't have anything to worry about. At least not right now."

That last addition to her declaration gave me hope that my friend might decide she deserved a better future.

"Besides, if Gideon does show," Nicole said. "He'll be looking for *you*."

She dropped into the driver's seat and closed the door before I could argue with her. But she was wrong if she thought a few seconds of delay would derail my response.

I climbed into the passenger seat and tucked my flowy skirt inside the car before I closed the door. I raised my brows at her. "Can we forget Gideon? If he shows, it will be because it's a big festival and he's in town. He won't be there for me. And let's just say that even if the world rolled over on its axis and he was interested, I'm not. I already have my life planned out, and it doesn't include a man. Not at my age."

Nicole chuckled. "What do a couple of hot chicks like us need with dumb guys anyway?"

I laughed, happy that she'd let go of the topic. "That's right. For forty-year-olds, we've still got it going on."

As if I'd ever had it going on. But it was fun to say. And for once, I did feel beautiful.

As we emerged onto Main Street, the lilac scented air was crisp with the vibrant spirit of the Beltane celebration. Winter had passed, and the season of fertility had begun. The world was fresh, and the atmosphere reminded me that life had been renewed. Anyone could cleanse their soul and start again with a new future if they chose to do so.

I felt more alive than I had in a while, and for a moment, I wondered how much I'd missed out on over the years. Practicing with a coven, using the combined energies and group-focused vitality of like-minded people sounded wonderful.

But then the enduring ache of knowing I didn't belong followed closely behind, which I promptly kicked to the curb. For the evening, anyway.

As we gazed ahead at the long row of booths and tents decorated in reds, whites, and greens, with people selling handcrafted jewelry, pottery, and lotions among other things, Nicole grabbed my hand in excitement. "Oh, look! Katelyn and her brother are here. Please, let's stop there first. I adore their honey so much."

"Let's do it," I said, doing my best to sound enthused. If I had to be at the festival, I did want to have a good time. "There's nothing like a cup of mint tea sweetened with Katelyn's clover honey on a chilly morning."

Nicole widened her eyes and nodded. "Exactly. I'm going to get one for your mom, too."

I appreciated that my friends had adopted my mom as their own, since their mothers lived so far away. "She'd love that."

Katelyn's smile widened when she caught sight of us approaching, and she waved us forward. My distant cousin had also missed out on the Summers' red hair, just like me, but her semi-short brown hair with blond highlights looked good with her square jawline. Plus, she did inherit the family's green eyes. "Ladies, you have to try this new lavender infused honey that my brother created. It's so good. I have some of Heather's fresh bread to try it with."

I was never one to pass up fresh bread with honey, so I happily stepped forward. There were subtle touches of witchcraft about her stall that a commoner wouldn't notice, like the bells hanging overhead for protection. I doubted any of the witches would steal from her, but there were always the other townsfolk. She'd also placed green jade near her cashbox for prosperity.

As I lifted a chunk of bread and the napkin it had been placed on, Katelyn held out a tiny plastic cup filled with honey. "It's so good to see you here this year, Daisy. I've missed you."

Guilt and warmth collided in my heart at the same time. There were a few of my coven sisters that I did enjoy seeing, but there was no reason I couldn't run into them in town, too. "Thanks, Katelyn. I'm happy to see you, too."

Nicole dunked her chunk of bread into the honey and plopped it into her mouth. A satisfied groan immediately filled the space around us. "Oh, my Goddess, Katelyn. This is divine."

Her brother Rory, who'd had his back to us, turned and grinned. He was a hard-working farmer with the muscles to prove it. His once completely dark hair had been woven with the silver telltale signs of getting older, but he was still handsome. "Thanks. I'm kind of proud of it."

As I dipped my bread into the honey, Nicole exclaimed. "You should be, Rory. It's delightful."

A blush stained his cheeks, and I remembered how much I'd liked the guy. I hadn't seen him for a few years, but he was still the same old, kind Rory that had been nice to everyone. I used to think he'd had a crush on Nicole in school, and his reaction to her comment made me wonder if he still did. They'd both married someone else, but from what I'd heard, Rory's marriage had also ended in divorce.

I didn't know if Nicole would be interested, but he was an upgrade from Cliff, in my opinion.

I placed the honey-drenched bread in my mouth and an exclamation of pleasure that sounded much like Nicole's escaped me. "Oh, wow. You're right. This *is* delicious. I'm glad we stopped here first because I bet that you'll run out before long."

Katelyn smiled, deepening the lines next to her eyes. "I said the same thing to Rory this morning. I wish we'd brought more, but we always have plenty of our clover honey as a backup. It will have to do."

I nodded and groaned as I finished chewing and swallowed the bread. "I'll take one of your regular honey and two of the lavender ones."

Nicole raised her hand. "Same. Actually, make that three with lavender because I want to take one to Daisy's mom."

Katelyn flicked her gaze to me. "How's your mom doing?"

I nodded. "Much better. She should be able to walk on her own very soon."

Katelyn tilted her head and cast a questioning look in my direction. "Hey, why aren't you doing a booth this year? Nothing like fresh bread and honey with one of your amazing coffees to wash it down."

I gave her an awkward smile, not wanting to explain my reluctance to join in. "Oh, I don't know. I guess I'd prefer to enjoy the evening looking at everyone else's stuff instead of selling my own."

Katelyn lifted a finger. "Good point. Luckily, I have Rory to help me set up and take down, not to mention watch the booth while I roam the area, too."

Nicole glanced at Katelyn's brother. "That's because Rory is one of the good guys."

This time, the blush reached to the tips of his ears in an endearing way. "Enough, ladies. It's not like I'm a saint. I can be a jerk, too."

I highly doubted that. Even from several feet away, I could sense the goodness in him.

"Never," Nicole agreed.

Katelyn wrapped the honey jars with paper before placing them in bags for us. "If you want some of Heather's bread, I'd go there next. You know she'll sell out, too. She's about six booths down."

I happily accepted my bag. "Thanks. That's exactly what we're going to do."

Nicole agreed with a nod. "Absolutely."

By the time we departed the booth, my spirits had lifted significantly. Maybe this evening wouldn't be so bad after all.

On the way to Heather's booth, we strolled past Geraldine and Mona's tent. The twin sister spinsters were selling Beltane flower crowns and bouquets, and I could smell the lilacs as we passed. If I was going to truly enjoy the night, I might as well go all in. I nudged Nicole. "I think I need one of those, too."

"For sure," she said. "After the bread."

I agreed. After all priorities were priorities.

I paid for and accepted the dense loaves of wheat and cranberry orange bread that Heather had bagged for me. "Mercy, these are not the fluffy white stuff."

Heather chuckled. "Nope. You'll only find the finest quality grains in my bread."

Nicole took the two that she'd purchased and weighed a loaf in each of her hands. "Then this must be the best bread ever because they are *heavy*."

The compliments brought a warm smile that encompassed Heather's whole face. "Fear not, ladies. The enchanted booth is open again this year. You can leave your purchases there without worry."

I'd completely forgotten the fair maintained such an area. The tradition had started many years ago when the festival had grown into what it was now. Witches had always brought their ritual tools with them for later, and at some point, someone had grown tired of carting them along with everything they'd purchased at the festival.

The booth was always cast with a spell so that no one except rightful owners could leave the area with anything that didn't belong to them. "That sounds fantastic, Nicole. Since we're already down this way, let's drop off our stuff before we buy flower crowns."

She grinned. "And when we head back, let's look for Gideon. I'm pretty sure I saw him."

I didn't answer in the affirmative, but I did swivel my head around for a quick glance in that direction.

SIX

Nicole led me to the enchanted booth at the end of the aisle of vendors. Lilibeth Summers, the teenaged daughter of a distant cousin leaned against a pole that held up the overhead heavy purple canvas that sparkled with printed gold stars. As we approached, Lilibeth laughed at whatever the blond young man standing very near to her had said.

When she caught me watching them, she lifted her hand in greeting. "Hi Aunt Daisy. Hi Nicole."

We exchanged greetings and then she took the guy's hand and led him off into the crowd. I got the distinct feeling that we'd somehow cramped her style.

Ahead of us, a white cloth with smaller gold stars covered the long folding table that separated the festival attendees from the booth attendant, who happened to be the sweet husband Fern had left behind.

Grover Jackson had his back to us as he placed bags into the wall of cubbies along the back of the booth. But then he turned, and I was sad to find that he still wasn't looking well. His long gray and white beard appeared more haggard than usual, and fresh grief shadowed his blue eyes even though Fern had departed to the other world over four months ago.

My heart went out to him. To lose a lifelong love must be such a shock. I gave him my kindest smile. "Hello, Grover. It's good to see you."

I wouldn't ask how he was doing because that was evident on his face.

His smile was genuine though. "Oh, Daisy. Nicole. You're a welcome sight."

Nicole reached out, and he took her hand. "Hello, Grover. You are, too. I know tonight will likely be difficult for you, but I'm glad that you're here with us."

He nodded solemnly. "Of course. My dearest Fern would want me to be here, to watch as her position is passed along to another."

Nicole squeezed his hand and released it. "She was a fabulous lady. Her shoes will be hard to fill."

He blinked several times, and I caught sight of moisture hovering in the corners of his eyes. "I just hope it goes to someone deserving."

I wanted to ask if he was worried that Merry might be chosen, but no sense adding to his distress. "I'm sure the Goddess will pick the best person."

Nicole nodded reassuringly, and he focused on me. "I hope that you're right. It could be you, you know, Daisy Mae."

I waved both hands in front of me as though that would dispel the Goddess's notion if that's what she'd intended. "No. Oh, no. That's not for me."

He lifted a shoulder and let it drop. "Could be anyone."

Anyone but me. And that was enough of that conversation. I set my heavy bags on the table between us. "Is it okay if we leave some stuff with you, Grover?"

"Of course," he said, tugging the sacks closer to him. He stood and placed them in one of the numbered cubbies that lined the booth's walls from ceiling to floor. He returned and wrote the number on a small piece of paper. "Number thirty-two for you."

Then he glanced at Nicole who shifted her gaze to me. "What about your cloak? Do you want to carry it around, too? I'm hot already, and I think I'll leave mine here until later."

I was nervous to part with the treasured article, but I wouldn't need it or my ritual tools until after midnight. No sense hauling them everywhere. "That's a good idea." I glanced at Grover. "I don't think it will fit with my other stuff. Can I use two spaces?"

He nodded, causing his long beard to brush halfway down the length of his torso. "By all means. Two cubbies for both of you."

He collected our items, placed them safely behind him in available spots, and returned to write the numbers for them. "You both have a pleasant evening. I'll see you when you return."

I gave him a grateful smile. "Thank you, Grover. Blessed be."

He and Nicole murmured the greeting, and I turned away, surprised that I was having a pleasant evening, indeed. Though I wasn't sure I'd tell my mom exactly how nice it had been. If I did, she'd be relentless in the coming years, and I wasn't certain I wanted to commit to any future events. Though maybe attending a celebration or a ritual occasionally might not be too bad if my friends were with me.

As Nicole and I turned back toward the flower booth, I spied the biggest reasons I'd avoided anything coven related. Merry, Oriana, and their two husbands were headed in our direction, and by the devious look hovering in Merry's eyes, I could tell she had already spotted me. As much as I wanted to escape, I wouldn't give her the pleasure of knowing my discomfort.

"Oh, no," Nicole whispered, and I knew she'd spotted them, too.

Oriana hung back from the rest of the group as they approached and glared at me with accusing disdain.

Merry stared at me as she neared, but her look carried a different vibe this time. She wasn't looking down on me. No, this time she looked at me with...*envy*.

It nearly shocked the strappy silver sandals I wore from my feet. Not once in my life had I encountered that reaction, but I couldn't describe it any other way. For that single moment, I was glad that I had visited my mother so that she could give me the dress and encourage me to beg my hair stylist to fit me in. All that fussing over what I'd considered nonsense now felt worth it.

Not that her emerald green dress wasn't beautiful, even though it was tight enough to threaten to spill her breasts from the bodice. Of course, her hair and makeup were perfect. But for once, it appeared she wanted what I had.

She placed a hand on her hip and gave me a sassy smile. "Well, look at you, Daisy."

Her husband Carl, who still had a full head of chestnut hair despite aging, lightly gripped her upper arm from behind and gave a gentle tug. "Merry," he cautioned in a whisper.

His reaction surprised me. I'd always thought he'd worshipped his wife and approved of her antics. But maybe that was no longer the case.

Merry pulled her arm free from his grasp, acting as though he'd never touched her.

I sent them all a smile full of light, if not love. "Blessed Beltane to you all."

She looked me up and down with disdain, but I caught her gaze lingering on my dress. "You actually did something with yourself."

Her words stunned me into silence.

Carl met my gaze and dipped his head in agreement. "I think you look very nice, Daisy."

I managed a smile. "Thank you, Carl."

Merry stepped backward, and Carl yelped in pain. I looked down to see that she'd firmly planted the heel of one of her shoes directly on his toes. In that moment, I felt sorry for Carl.

He pushed Merry aside, and she wobbled in her heels, making me wonder if she'd started drinking early. He looked at the rest of his small group. "I'm going to get a beer."

Carl didn't wait for anyone to reply before he stomped off.

Oriana moved in closer and turned to her husband with questioning eyes. "Do you want one, too, Bill? I'll go get you one if you do."

He looked from Merry to his wife, almost seeming annoyed that she'd bothered him. "Sure. Grab me a beer. Maybe two so that I don't have to go back later."

I'd never cared for Bill's less than charming attitude, and once again, I was reminded why.

Oriana nodded to Bill and then paused, pointing two fingers at her eyes, and then directing them toward me in a warning that said she'd be watching me. Then she turned away and headed off in the direction Carl had taken.

Merry inhaled a deep breath and gave me an icy smile. "Looks like I was right about you not finding a date, too. You can frost a cupcake, but you'll still have the same, dry old cake underneath."

Bill snorted, and I caught the snarky grin on his face.

"Merry," Nicole said in a disapproving tone, warning her.

But she didn't need to protect me. I'd decided the moment I'd seen Merry's face that she would not ruin this night for me.

Merry opened her mouth as if to speak, but then closed it. I'd wondered what had caused her change of heart until I realized she was now looking beyond my shoulder. She twisted her lips into a seductive smile. "Well, hello, newcomer. Welcome to the Sweet Mountain Meadows May Day celebration."

I looked over my shoulder to find Gideon McKay standing just behind me, looking quite handsome in a white button-down shirt that flowed loosely around him. The blue jeans and dark boots only added to his sexy look.

Unfortunately, he'd shown up just in time to hear more of Merry's insults, and I gave an inward groan.

SEVEN

Gideon's gaze immediately shifted to me, and I felt the weight of his appraisal. "Hi, my lovely. Sorry that it took me so long. The line for flower crowns was quite lengthy."

Before I could question what he'd meant, he produced two crowns, one made with white daisies, and the other crafted from lilacs and tiny pink roses. He handed the colorful one to Nicole, and she grinned. "Why, thank you, Gideon. That's very generous of you."

He gave a slight bow in response and turned his gaze to me. "This one is for you. Daisies for my lovely Daisy."

A tingle of awareness flitted through me as he placed the crown of white flowers on my head. His gift had caught me so off guard that it took me a moment to gather my wits. He must not be aware of the meaning of giving such a gift. As far as lore went, giving daisies to a woman was a way for a man to know if she loved him in return. To give them at Beltane, the celebration of new beginnings...

I pushed away those thoughts, because, of course, he wouldn't know anything about that. "It's beautiful. Thank you."

He turned to Merry and Bill and dipped his head. "If you'll excuse us, I promised these lovely ladies that I'd treat them to mead and honey cakes. Traditional food for Beltane, I believe."

The fact that he'd called the celebration by its correct name instead of May Day impressed me. I sent Merry my sweetest smile. "Yes, excuse us."

Nicole echoed my sentiment, and Gideon held out an arm for each of us. I didn't need him to rescue me from Merry, but I didn't mind it, either.

When we were a fair distance away, I glanced up at Gideon. "Thank you for that. She can be a beast sometimes."

"All the time," Nicole corrected.

Gideon chuckled. "I surmised that from earlier in the coffee shop. Not to mention, she does carry a dark air about her."

A dark air? I studied his profile with interest. "I'll admit that I've sensed something dark about you, as well. Something that carries an air of magic, but nothing nasty like Merry. I have to ask, are you a witch?"

He chuckled, and the deep, rich sound traveled all the way to my toes. "No, no. Not a witch."

Nicole waved at Grover as we passed the enchanted booth again, and then she tilted her head as she regarded Gideon. "So, not a witch, but you don't deny the magic?"

As we squeezed through an area crowded with people waiting in lines on both sides of the walkway, he tugged me closer to him. "Yes, I would say that I do have a kind of magic, but let's leave it at that, shall we?"

I blinked in surprise, wondering if he was one of the Fae who supposedly could visit on Beltane. Of course, I didn't want to appear rude and press a man that I'd just met for more information. We were, after all, only acquaintances at a public event, but I was curious. "Well, thank you for rescuing us, but don't feel obligated to treat us to mead and honey cakes. You've already been too kind."

His gaze met mine. "As it happens, I'm free for the rest of the evening. Would you mind if I joined you after all? My presence has the added benefit of keeping Merry away from you."

Unfortunately, before I could find an excuse as to why he couldn't, Nicole beamed at him. "That would be lovely."

He looked at me to see if I also agreed.

What could I say at that point? "Of course."

His smile glowed with happiness, and we continued through the crowd of people toward the town square where food and drink were served.

As we walked, Nicole twirled her fingers through the pink and lavender ribbons that drifted down from her crown and hung over her shoulder. "I know I'm repeating myself, but thank you again, Gideon. I haven't received this beautiful of a gift in a long time."

"Doesn't your boyfriend spoil you?" he asked, and I was surprised that he knew about Cliff.

Nicole gave a soft snort. "No, he seems to be lacking in that area."

That and many others.

The only thing I could think of was that Nicole must have told him about Cliff when Gideon had been in the shop earlier and visiting the kitties. He *had* been in the Purry Parlor for over an hour, after all.

Nicole had made it seem like she hadn't told him much, but I feared her declaration had been an exaggeration. Though she couldn't have told him I'd be at the festival because I hadn't decided if I'd go yet, so he couldn't be there on my account.

Still, I knew there was more to this Mr. Gideon McKay, and I found myself wanting to learn what that might be.

EIGHT

A n hour later, I'd consumed one and a half glasses of mead and was already feeling tipsy. I'd forgotten that Old Man Jeffers had often boasted about the potency of his fermented honey concoctions, but by the time I remembered, it was too late. I couldn't undo what had been done.

Aeri and her husband had joined us, adding to the jovial atmosphere. They'd been very welcoming to Gideon, and I appreciated that.

They were the most handsome couple I knew. Her with her deep brown hair and eyes, dressed in a pale green dress that would be the envy of any fairies who'd snuck into our realm for the night, and Brad with his styled blond hair looking dapper, who only had eyes for Aeri.

I knew I'd made up my mind to be happy with the simple life consisting of my cafe and kitties, but I couldn't deny that I envied their connection. Though I was also wise enough to know those kinds of relationships were rare.

The heat from the two bonfires burning in the center of the town square to celebrate fertility and new life crackled and popped. They were close enough that I felt the heat on my back, and I wondered if that intensified the mead's effects. Of course, it didn't help that the wild energy emanating from the Celtic Band who played an Irish jig sent my pulse racing.

Regardless of the cause, I found myself completely relaxed and having a great time. Many had complimented me on my dress and my hair, and I'd begun to feel like the belle of the ball. I knew it was only for one night, but that was okay. Tomorrow, things would go back to normal, but the rareness of feeling pretty and having a handsome man amongst our group who seemed inclined to give me a fair share of the attention was another form of intoxication that I wasn't entirely immune to.

Unfortunately, Merry and her group sat only two tables away, and more than once I'd caught her staring at Gideon.

We'd all finished laughing at one of Brad's jokes when Gideon reached over and placed his hand on mine. "Dance with me, Daisy."

A shock ricocheted through my system, and I immediately declined without considering my answer. "Thanks, but I'm not much of a dancer. I bet Nicole would like to, though."

He looked at Nicole and lifted his brow.

She grinned and nodded. "I'd love to."

They both stood, and he leaned down to whisper in my ear. "I will dance this one with your friend, but the next slow song will be for me and you."

He didn't give me a chance to argue before he walked away with his hand on Nicole's back, guiding her to the paved cobblestone area in front of the band where many people danced to the music.

A shiver raced through me. In an effort to cool myself, I took a long drink of the second glass of mead in front of me and leaned back against my chair. I couldn't help but wonder if I was dreaming.

Everything around me swirled together, the music, the fires that crackled to the beat, the mead that burned in my belly, and the carefree laughter of loved ones. My mother had been right. The night was special. Something to be soaked up and cherished in future days when life was more mundane.

Near the end of the song, Nicole returned to the table alone.

I lifted my brows. "Where's Gideon?"

She turned a knowing gaze in my direction, as though to confirm that she'd been right regarding my interest in him. "He said he'd be right back."

And he was. He returned just as the band's music drifted into an eerie, yet seductive slower song about a woman walking along the ocean, waiting for her lover to return. He didn't bother to sit but held his hand out to me. "Shall we?"

Every head at the table turned to me, and alcohol-infused heat raced to my cheeks. Luckily, evening had fallen and my distress wouldn't be so obvious amongst the flickers of firelight and shadows. My first instinct was to deny him again, but something foreign inside me lifted me out of my chair and placed my hand into Gideon's. He gave it a light squeeze, sending a rush of attraction straight to my core.

I hoped the Blessed Goddess was looking out for me. I knew I was vulnerable to him, but that didn't stop me. At least I knew that my friends, who were good at sensing the true nature of people, liked him.

As we danced, Gideon held me close, his arm around my waist and mine on his shoulder. His cologne tickled my senses, and I found him to be the perfect dance partner. Not that I was, but he made me seem so.

He stared into my eyes. "Thank you for an enchanting evening, lovely Daisy."

The man had finesse. I'd give him that. "My thanks to you, too. I've enjoyed your company...everyone's company tonight as well."

An amused grin curved his lips when I added that last bit to my reply.

I didn't want him to think he had me completely charmed.

But then I worried that he might have taken it as a slight, which I hadn't meant it to be. "It's definitely a fairytale night," I added quickly to soften the meaning, but then I realized I was rambling, which didn't help anything.

He tilted his head as he perused my face and then moved his gaze outward toward my hair and the crown of daisies on my head. "A fairytale, and you're the princess."

I was about to deny his comment when someone grabbed my upper arm and turned me with enough force to cause me to stumble. Gideon tightened his grip on my waist and gave my accoster an annoyed frown.

I shouldn't have been surprised that it was Merry. A drunk, wobbling Merry. She stared at Gideon with undeniable lust. "Mind if I cut in?"

I dropped my jaw, unable to speak, but Gideon answered for me. "Actually, yes. This is our first dance together, and I'd like to finish it."

Merry snorted. "Why?" She placed a hand on Gideon's forearm to steady herself. "Why have her, when you could have me instead?"

Many of the couples around us stopped to watch the drama, dropping dread into my stomach and tightening it. I looked up at Gideon, wanting to lessen the tension. I didn't want to let Merry win, but the need to be out of the limelight was stronger. "It's fine if you do. I'll just be back at the table."

I tried to pull away, but he refused to let go. "No, it's not fine."

He turned to Merry. "Please leave us, Ms. Mercer."

Anger colored her features. "But...but...we have a deal."

He snorted. "That's a business deal. Nothing personal."

She shook her head, not at all happy with his reply. Luckily, her husband had found his way to her through the gathering of people. "Merry. Stop it."

She turned to him with a look of disgust so rabid that it made me flinch. "Take your hands off me," she commanded just as the song ended.

Carl cast glances about him, obviously embarrassed. "Pardon us. She's a little drunk." He wrapped a firm hand around her upper arm. "Come on, darling. I have a surprise for you."

Merry brightened. "A surprise? Oh, I love surprises."

He led her off then without much resistance.

Gideon turned to me and lifted my chin with his forefinger. "I apologize for that."

"Apologize? I think it's my fault she's acting the way she is."

The band started up again, and people seemed content to return to their activities.

He took my hand and led me away from the paved area and into the shadows of nearby trees. I went willingly, grateful to be away from curious eyes.

He stopped and turned to me. "Why would you think it's your fault?"

I couldn't put into words how much my pretty dress, my fun evening, my happiness bothered Merry, so I shrugged instead.

He stared at me for a moment and then nodded. "I see."

I widened my eyes. How could he? "You do?"

It was his turn to shrug. "You're easy for me to read."

I dropped my head and groaned. The last thing I needed was for this handsome man to know my insecurities. I returned my gaze to him. "She's been a thorn in my side since the day I was born."

He lifted a finger. "Except her reaction isn't all about you. Perhaps, it's the combination of us being together."

Together? We were together? I mean, we might have danced, but we weren't together-together. "What do you mean?"

His lips curved into a smile that didn't reach his eyes. "I'm in town for business. To discuss a proposition with Merry."

I knew that Carl and Merry had many business holdings but most were investments in local properties, and Carl had always handled the details. "What kind of business?"

He flicked a glance beyond me, back toward the festival, and shook his head. "It's not important now. The papers have been signed and should be finalized soon. There's really no reason for me to have anything further to do with her. She obviously has a problem with self-awareness and boundaries."

His reply coaxed a chuckle from me, and he seemed pleased about that. "Yes," I agreed. "Among many other issues."

My watch buzzed, and I glanced at it. "It's close to midnight."

"Ah. Well then, we'll have to finish our dance another time. I believe you have an important ritual to attend."

I decided that because he was a magical person of some sort and aware that we celebrated Beltane, he would know the coven would hold a ritual. "Yes. There will be a passing down of a legacy, in addition to other things."

He took my hand and wrapped it around his arm, keeping his fingers on top as though to prevent me from escaping. "Let's get you back to your friends, then."

We didn't speak again as he escorted me to the table. He shook Brad's hand and kissed each of us ladies on the cheek. "Thank you all for letting me crash your party. It was a pleasure."

Nicole widened her eyes into a bright look. "I hope we'll see you again."

He nodded. "Of course. I'll likely be in the coffee shop a few more times before I leave town."

The notion that my chances of seeing him again were limited brought a sadness I couldn't explain. "Thank you for the evening, Gideon."

He caught my gaze, and something dark and mysterious rippled through me. He smiled, nodded, and walked away.

I couldn't help watching him until he disappeared into the crowd.

Brad cleared his throat. "I think Daisy may have met her match."

I swiveled my head toward him even as heat scalded my cheeks. I scoffed. "Then you thought wrong. He's a very nice man, and yes, he's interesting. But he's only here for a few days on business, and you know I'm not looking for a serious relationship with anyone."

Aeri and Nicole shared a look that irritated me. "Stop, will you? Let's collect our things and head to the woods. I'd like to get there early and pick a spot in the circle where we can make a quick exit once they announce Fern's replacement. I don't think I can stand to watch Merry gloat."

Nicole slipped her arm through mine, and we made our way back to the enchanted tent. "It could be you," she whispered, teasing me.

I looked her directly in the eye. "No."

NINE

As far as celebrations went, Beltane was one of my favorites, preceded only by Samhain. During this special time halfway between Ostara, the spring equinox, and Litha, the midsummer solstice, our coven along with witches around the world celebrated the turning of the wheel into the season where life thrived once again. It gave me renewed hope for humanity and myself.

Nicole, Aeri, and I retrieved our items from Grover and snagged two lanterns from the cluster that he'd lit and placed on the table for ceremonial use. We said goodbye to Brad since men were not allowed to attend the ritual unless they possessed magical powers, which rarely happened throughout history. In fact, there had never been a male witch in our coven.

From there, the lanterns cast light around us as we followed the well-worn path into the trees. The calming scents of pine and earth filled the cool evening air, and our feet crunched twigs and pinecones as we walked. I donned the soft white wool cloak that had once belonged to my great grandmother, and Aeri gasped. "My, my, my. That is a beautiful robe. Where ever did you get it?"

The excitement that Merry had banished with her appearance emerged once again, and a rush of delicious energy washed through me. I swore I sensed some of Aibreann's power still lingering in the threads of the fabric. "My mom gave it to me. It belonged to my great grandmother many times over."

Aeri lifted her brows in astonishment. "Amazing. Your mother had it all this time?"

I shrugged. "Passed down through generations of witches to me."

Nicole snorted. "That right there proves that your bloodline isn't dead. There's no way that robe would have made it to you, otherwise."

Aeri chuckled. "You're going to be the next to be chosen, Daisy. Just watch."

I had to admit things had lined up in a crazy fashion that night, but I still couldn't consider that it might happen. I wouldn't be disappointed though. In fact, I'd be relieved. The wonderful evening with amazing people, good food, and fun was enough to bring me happiness for years. It might even encourage me to get out more from time to time.

As we walked through the darkened woods that whispered as the wind passed through the new leaves, I focused on the good memories of Beltane and the fun feelings I'd had earlier that evening, pushing aside the awkwardness of Merry's interruption and the fact that Gideon would soon be leaving town. It had been a special night, and I intended to finish it out the way it had started. My Cinderella time was almost over, but not quite yet.

I linked arms with my friends and smiled. "Let's make this the best Beltane ritual ever."

They both laughed and agreed.

Oriana and Jocelyn, the high priestess of our coven, were already at the clearing when we arrived at the circle of grass amongst the trees. The ritual bonfire snapped and popped, sending light into the dark shadows, and I knew Jocelyn would have arrived early to start it along with making other preparations. It would have been rude for me not to approach and wish them well, so I allowed my friends to move me forward until we faced them. "Merry meet," I said and dipped my head.

The others responded in kind even though I felt and saw the irate disbelief shimmering in Oriana's eyes. I was tempted to call her out and ask her what her problem was, even though I knew. But I didn't want to spoil the evening. I wasn't, however, about to ask her where her sister was. The less I saw of Merry, the better.

At some point though, maybe after the ceremony, I would talk to Oriana to let her know that I didn't appreciate being called a liar and a thief.

Jocelyn eyed my cloak, widening her eyes as she did. "Beautiful robe, Daisy."

Awkwardness crept over me from her scrutiny. "Thank you. My mother gifted it to me today. A family heirloom."

A hint of a smile quirked the corners of Jocelyn's mouth. "Oh, aye. I do recognize it from paintings. If I'm correct, it once belonged to Aibreann."

Oriana lifted her brows in shocked surprise, because Aibreann was also her grandmother of old. That expression was quickly replaced by suspicion and envy. "How did you end up with it?" she asked, sounding petty as she spoke, probably thinking I'd stolen it as well.

I lifted my head a little higher, knowing that this gift was much more prized than the ring she'd claimed I'd stolen. Not that I wouldn't have been appreciative if that had been given to me instead. But this robe made a grand statement that suddenly made me very proud. "Down the line," I said, emphasizing the word. "From Aibreann to other grandmothers to my mother to me."

I knew it wasn't humble to brag about my gift, but I'd been squashed for too long, and Oriana and her sister had been the worst offenders.

Amusement flickered in Jocelyn's eyes. "You wear it well."

We finished our greetings, and as we walked away, I heard Oriana ask the high priestess if it could be a fake. "Oh, no," she responded. "Did you not feel the magic pulsating from it?"

"No," Oriana responded in a quiet voice.

Jocelyn clucked. "You must work on purifying your spirit of negativity to be in alignment then, dear one."

The wise old crone's words left me with a grin.

Aeri, Nicole, and I settled onto the soft grass along the edge of the circle and began to remove our ritual items. I pulled the small, traveling chalice from my bag and set it on the grass in front of me. I'd received it as a gift from Katelyn's mother years ago. I loved the way the silver finish caught the firelight and made it easy to see the delicate etching around the cup. I had decided a while back that I would gift it back to one of Katelyn's children when I grew older.

I reached into the other pocket to retrieve my ritual knife and froze. A sense of loss slithered over me, but I refused to accept it. "My athame," I whispered, reaching deep into the cloak's pocket, searching every inch of it. When I found nothing, I stuffed my hand into the other pocket where I'd stored my chalice.

Nothing.

Nicole tilted her head toward me. "What's wrong?"

A small surge of panic rolled through me. "My knife. It's missing."

"Missing?" Aeri echoed. "Are you sure you brought it?"

I nodded fervently. "Yes, I'm certain. I placed my chalice and my athame in my pockets at the same time."

Nicole reached into the pocket closest to her. "There couldn't be a hole, could there?"

"No," I said. "I just checked."

It wasn't as if my knife was particularly special like my chalice, other than it had served me well, and I didn't want to lose it. I'd purchased it at a fair years ago, and although I did love the design, it had never felt perfectly right in my hand. Unfortunately, it did have some monetary value because of the large peridot embedded into the shaft, so if someone not magical found it, I likely wouldn't see it again. "I guess it could have slipped out while I was walking into the festival, but I was very careful."

Nicole placed a comforting hand on my forearm. "It's okay. I can help you with mine."

"And who knows," Aeri added. "It might turn up."

I frowned and forced myself to accept that it was a minor thing compared to everything else that evening. Nicole's knife would work just fine.

Other members flooded in as the clock ticked closer to midnight. At the stroke of the hour, Jocelyn stood near the bonfire in the center of the circle and glanced at each of us. All voices immediately quieted, and an air of spirituality filtered amongst us.

Mona, one of the spinster flower ladies with bright orange hair, walked the circle, sprinkling salt as she did. Jocelyn called to each of the elements to watch over us and protect us during our ritual.

I felt the Goddess's deep love as we honored a moment of silence where we quietly reviewed the past year, our failures and successes, and then wrote our intentions for the coming season. Once we'd finished, we tossed our papers into the flames and let our wishes ride the smoke into the heavens.

The high priestess led us in song, and our voices blended beautifully as we sang of lovers and wild mountain thyme.

After a while, Jocelyn took her place near the center of the circle and slowly turned, glancing once again at each of our faces. I swore she hesitated when she met my gaze, but then she continued. "We've now reached the portion of our ritual where we will learn who the goddess has chosen to join our esteemed council. Dear Fern, bless her departed soul, was a gifted witch, an honored member of our coven, and a dedicated mentor who shared her knowledge with all. I know I speak for all of us when I say we will miss her."

Whispers of agreement drifted from the circle of women.

"But as goes the cycle of life," Jocelyn continued. "We must bless her and move forward with our work."

She bent to retrieve the small cast-iron cauldron resting near her. "I've placed the names of all witches from the appropriate line dating back to the beginning of our coven."

Murmurs and speculations of who would be chosen rolled through the group, and Aeri reached over to squeeze my hand. I wanted to ask her to stop because she was making me more nervous. Not that I didn't appreciate her support, but it was unwarranted.

Jocelyn lifted a stick from the ground and held it out to the fire until the flames caught hold. She held it high into the air. "Blessed Goddess, we call upon thee. Our coven desires someone to lead. Show us this person, so mote it be."

Then she placed the tip of the burning twig into the cauldron and smoke emerged.

The high priestess waited a moment before she accepted a chalice of water from Mona who stood nearby, and she poured the contents into the cauldron. Holding a lantern overhead, Jocelyn gazed inside, then swirled her hand around until she pulled from it a piece of soaked but not burned paper.

Strings of tension weaved throughout the coven members and grew taut as Jocelyn focused on the paper. She blinked, and looked once again at the gathering. Then she focused her gaze directly at me.

Reality cracked, and my insides tightened as all air left my body.

"The Goddess chooses Daisy Summers."

TEN

Chaos erupted amidst the coven members, and the inability to draw a proper breath left me faint.

Nicole threw her arms around me in excitement, and we both nearly toppled over. "I knew it!"

Aeri joined the group hug, adding her enthusiastic energy to Nicole's. "Oh, Daisy. I'm so happy for you. This is the best thing ever."

Other people began to crowd around, heightening my anxiety. "No," I whispered to my friends. "This isn't okay."

Aeri was the first to lean back and study me. Concern darkened her eyes, and I sensed when she picked up on my emotions. "What's wrong?" she asked in a low voice.

Fear caused my stomach to clench. "I don't want this. It's not meant for me."

Nicole gave me a quiet smile. "Yes, dear. It is. The Goddess has spoken. Will you deny her?"

I...I couldn't. Not if I believed in my faith, which I did wholeheartedly. "There must be a mistake."

Aeri shook her head. "The Goddess doesn't make mistakes."

I caught sight of the high priestess as she moved past several people, walking closer to me. When she reached the circle of my friends and me, she touched Nicole on the shoulder. Nicole immediately stepped back to make room for her.

Jocelyn tossed her long silver braid over her shoulder, and I noted that her hair was not unlike the way I usually wore mine. I found knowledge when I gazed into her bright blue, almost purple eyes. And perhaps a hint of amusement.

She held out a hand wrinkled by time, and I automatically wrapped my fingers around it. White, powerful energy surged into me, reminding me that this lady wasn't one to trifle with. "Daisy Summers. Look at you. I knew someday you would blossom."

Had I blossomed? I felt more like I'd withered under her and everyone's stares. I wanted to say something, but I couldn't find the right words.

Jocelyn dipped her head as though acknowledging what I wasn't saying. "The Goddess has offered you a gift."

A gift that felt more like a noose. Beyond Jocelyn, I found Oriana and Katelyn watching me with intense eyes. I turned my gaze back to Jocelyn because I didn't think I could handle Merry's expression if she was somewhere close by.

I inhaled a shaky breath but remained mute. I had no clue what a person said in times like these.

A daring smile played on Jocelyn's lips. "As above, so below, Daisy. What is your answer?"

She'd reminded me that everything is connected, and all witches should want a balanced world. Was that why the Goddess had chosen me? Had our coven become unbalanced?

As much as I wanted to, I could not deny fate. "I accept."

Oriana released a cry of dismay that everyone surely heard. She lifted a lantern and ran off into the trees, heading back toward the town square. Obviously, she wasn't pleased with the outcome.

Not far from where she entered the forest, I found Gideon standing amongst the shadows, leaning against the thick trunk of an old bur oak tree. His gaze connected with mine, and he smiled.

Who or what was he?

The sounds of clapping and offers of congratulations drew my attention back to my surroundings.

Jocelyn leaned in and kissed my cheek. "Congratulations, dear. I sense your reservations, but know that I have complete faith in you. Now, let us celebrate."

She grasped the light blue prismatic pendant hanging around her neck on a long chain and slipped it over her head. She held it out toward me, and I bowed my head to receive it.

"I gift to you this celestite to protect and guide you in the years to come. A mentor gave it to me the day I was chosen to serve. I feel called to pass it along to you."

I placed my hand over the crystal, sensing the protection of an unseen force. Knowing that pure energy would be on my side to guide me eased my fears considerably.

I pictured the excitement on my mom's face, and a wisp of happiness filtered in. She would be thrilled, and she deserved all the happiness that could be found in her later years.

With that, the high priestess left my side, drawing Aeri and Nicole with her. Soon, other members of the coven crowded in, each of them offering their congratulations. Some, I sensed, were heartfelt and encouraging, while others were wary and some downright fake.

Grover pushed his way through to me and took my hand. He must have also been watching from a distance. His fingers were cold, and sadness emanated from him. He seemed to have become much more tired since I'd last seen him at the enchanted booth. But I expected the choice of a replacement for his dearly departed wife would take a toll.

He squeezed my hand and met my gaze with watery eyes. "This choice would please Fern. As you know, she was very devoted to the coven, to balance amongst all, and to kindness. I know that you possess all of those qualities, so my heart can be at peace."

I blinked back my own tears, touched by his sentiments. "Thank you, Grover. That means a lot to me."

He reached into his coat and produced a black-handled athame that was sheathed in black leather which had been tooled with the Tree of Life, a Celtic symbol for balance. "I have no use for this," he said. "No children to pass it along to, so I would like to gift it to you. I hope that whenever you use it, you'll sense Fern's loving spirit there with you."

I wanted to tell him no, that it was too precious, and he should keep it to remind him of Fern, but I could see that this was important to him. I opened my palms, and he placed the knife across them both. "Blessed be," I whispered, wishing peace and comfort to him.

"Blessed be," he repeated, bowed his head, and turned away.

I did a quick search for Aeri and Nicole, needing my friend's presence to bolster me, but they'd gathered in a circle with Jocelyn and listened intently as she spoke to them.

A small part of me wondered if she'd drawn them away on purpose.

Katelyn was the next to greet me. I was certain she was disappointed that she hadn't been chosen, but I didn't tell her that I wished she had been as well.

I held out my hand to her, and she took it. "Congratulations, Daisy." She lifted a small potted rosemary plant. "Blessings for health and wellness. If there's anything you require of me, I'll do my best to help you."

I was deeply grateful for her gift, and I hope she sensed that. "Thank you, Katelyn."

Mona, the friendly, if not smart, older stepped forward, and I glanced down so that I could meet her gaze.

Before we had a chance to speak, a gut-wrenching wail echoed through the night and pierced the happy bubble that had surrounded the circle. Mona's eyes grew wide, and a frigid chill fell over me. I glanced toward the high priestess and my friends who all stared toward the woods.

The cry had silenced the coven, and everyone glanced about as though wondering what to do.

Jocelyn lifted a hand. "Let's remain calm. Some of us, perhaps all of us should head in that direction to see what's happened. Safety in numbers." She flicked a glance at Nicole. "Perhaps an emergency call to police is in order as well."

Nicole nodded quickly and pulled out her phone as everyone gathered into a group and headed into the woods.

It didn't take us long to find the cause of the awful cry.

A lantern sat along the edge of a small clearing, casting dancing shadows on the scene before it. Oriana knelt over someone lying supine on the soft grass. She stared in horror at the small knife she held in her hand, and it took only a second for me to realize the blade was covered with blood.

Someone screamed, and I gasped.

Only then did Oriana turn her gaze toward us. Shock colored her expression, and her hand shook as she held out the weapon. *"Someone's stabbed my sister."*

Fear rippled through the group. Jocelyn, being the amazing leader that she was, strode forward and knelt next to Merry. Her hand shook as she reached out to Merry's neck to check for a pulse.

A moment later, she turned to Nicole. "You'd better follow up that call with another to let them know we may have a murderer on the loose."

ELEVEN

An eerie sensation swirled around me as we stood gaping at the horrific scene. It cut through the hushed whispers from those standing nearby, and I had the distinct impression that Merry was still with us. And that she was angry. Very angry.

I couldn't blame her for being incensed. If someone had taken my life before I was ready to leave this earth, I'd be furious, too.

Then a second later, all traces of that sensation disappeared, and I assumed Merry had passed to the next realm.

I stared in disbelief at her body and at Oriana kneeling over her. Oriana had said someone had stabbed her sister. I couldn't help but wonder if that person was her. After all, she was holding the obvious murder weapon.

My blood chilled at the thought, and I drew my cloak closer around me the best that I could while still holding the potted rosemary. I tried to get a read on Oriana's emotions and found nothing but shock. No sadness. No guilt. I wondered at the lack of sadness, thinking, surely, Oriana would be somewhat distraught over losing her sister. Not that Merry had been particularly good to her, but the two were often seen together. Oriana couldn't have hated her that much. Could she?

Nicole and Aeri scooted close to me and threaded their arms through mine. We stayed linked like that until the police arrived. Thankfully, it didn't take them long.

Three officers arrived on scene first. Two men and one woman. They quickly assessed Merry, I guess to make sure she was dead, and then they turned on us. As far as I could tell, none seemed too friendly toward witches. Some of the town's residents who knew that we met in the forest on occasion misunderstood what we believed and what we were about. I feared these officers were among them.

I recognized the tall, strawberry blond female, Sofia, who happened to be one of my customers, though she was usually out of uniform when she came into the shop. She strode toward the gathering of witches as we huddled together, and my insides tightened into a bigger ball of nerves. She pulled a notepad from a pocket in her jacket and cleared her throat to capture our attention. As if she needed to. We were already freaked out and focused on her.

Sofia glanced at each of us. When her gaze fell on me, she lifted her brow as though letting me know she was surprised to find me there. Which she probably was, since I was what the coven called a closet witch.

Or at least I had been. Things would be different now, I expected, and I hoped it wouldn't cost me customers.

"Uh...ladies?" Sofia said as though she was unsure of how to address us. I nodded because the term was, indeed, appropriate. We weren't Satanists for Hades' sake.

Sofia drew a circle in the air. "This area is now officially a crime scene. We need a statement from each of you, but we will conduct those interviews back in town in a more comfortable setting. Before we head back, though, I need to collect your names just in case someone accidentally slips off into the night without giving us information."

Mona was the only one to chuckle, but it was a nervous one, and I was sure she didn't find our situation the slightest bit funny.

Sofia moved to the back of the group, away from Merry's body, and we all turned to follow her as she went. She pointed to Mona. "We'll start with you, ma'am. Give me your full name and phone number."

Mona scoffed and pushed her hood back to reveal a mop of gray hair. "It's me, Sofia. Don't act like you don't know me. Your grandmama and I have been friends since the beginning of time."

Sofia seemed to shrink a little. "Sorry, Mrs. Thompson. I'm just following procedures."

Mona gave a lofty exhale and spoke her name and number. Sofia quickly wrote them down. Then she lifted her gaze to the older witch. "If you'd be so kind, please step aside while I gather other names. Then we'll head back to town as a group."

Mona seemed appeased by her concern, nodded, and moved away.

Sofia was a fast writer, and it didn't take her long to get to me and my friends. She briefly blinded us with her flashlight as we approached. To get a good look at our faces, I expected. Perhaps she was even looking for signs of guilt. Which would make sense. Which also left me feeling more nervous than before. Because now I probably did look guilty.

"Hi Sofia," I said before giving my information, just to, you know, let her know that we were also friends, and that I'd never do anything so heinous as to commit murder.

She didn't seem impressed and treated me like everyone else.

Maybe that was a good thing.

When everyone had given their names, Sofia appointed Jocelyn to lead us through the forest, while she followed up from behind. Aeri, Nicole, and I stayed close as we trod across the dirt path covered with old leaves and pine needles.

Shadows seemed to move and dart about us. I tried to convince myself that my imagination played tricks on me and that a murderer didn't lurk amongst them. But I couldn't forget there was a devious soul somewhere nearby, perhaps even walking near me, so one couldn't be too careful.

Back in town, Sofia led us to the town square where the fires still burned brightly, sending plumes of smoke into the night. Earlier, the flames had seemed so cheerful and happy. Now, it felt more like the fires of Hades licked at my feet.

Sofia directed everyone to find a seat in the general area, and I found us heading toward the table where we'd sat earlier. As I planted my bottom on the cold, metal chair, I wished we'd sat somewhere else. I wanted to remember this table as it had been, filled with happiness and laughter. Not tainted by Merry's death.

Thoughts of Gideon filtered in, and my stomach clenched when I realized he'd been near our circle in the forest right around the time Merry had been murdered. I'd caught sight of him when Jocelyn had announced my name, and he'd seemed pleased for me. But I hadn't seen him since.

Had he left the area before Oriana had found Merry? Or was there a darker reason he wasn't among us now?

I shivered.

Aeri must have noticed my stress because she reached over and patted my hand. "I feel it, too, Daisy. A darkness amongst us, and I don't like it."

"Me, either," Nicole added.

A darkness? I'd used that sentiment earlier when I'd appraised the energy Gideon carried. He hadn't seemed evil to me, but there had been something dark.

Two more male officers arrived to help Sofia with our statements, one of whom had been my secret crush so many years ago. I couldn't help but watch Corey Shelton as he walked to the table where Katelyn and her friend sat, and he urged Katelyn to follow him with a crook of his finger.

Twenty-five years ago, I would have followed that invitation anywhere. Of course, Corey hadn't been aware of the teenage crush I'd had on him. In fact, most guys hadn't given me a second look because they'd all known that I'd come from a broken line, and they wanted to be with the popular girls who had a chance of becoming powerful and important one day.

Still, I'd always thought Corey was handsome with his dark curly hair and quick smile. Not to mention he'd been taller than me, which most of the guys my age hadn't been at that time.

When Corey took the last person from Katelyn's table, it created distance between my group and the others still waiting for their turn. Aeri turned to me. The flames that danced behind me mirrored in her eyes, and I found fear lingering there.

Her expression churned my own sense of dread. "What's wrong, Aeri? Other than the obvious."

Aeri moistened her bottom lip as she studied me. "I probably shouldn't say anything."

Which was a stupid thing for her to reveal now that she had my attention. "Of course, you should. Otherwise, I won't sleep tonight."

Nicole frowned. "Me, either, Aeri. Spill it."

Aeri exhaled a slow breath. "That's the problem. I'm afraid if I do tell you then you won't sleep for a long time."

Nicole huffed. "Too late. Just say it already."

Aeri started to speak. Stopped. And then continued. "I'm not certain, okay? But I *think* the knife that Oriana held was yours, Daisy."

I inhaled so sharply that I choked. *"What? No."*

Nicole widened her eyes in despair, and Aeri sent us both an apologetic look. "I'm sorry. I probably shouldn't have said anything until we know for sure, but I...saw a yellow green stone, a peridot near the hilt. It was mostly covered in blood, but—"

Aeri shrugged in apology.

I couldn't respond. I could barely breathe.

That simply couldn't be.

I was about to ask Nicole if she'd noticed the peridot, too, but the flames behind me cast a dark shadow over our table, and I felt a presence nearby. I turned to see Corey standing over my shoulder. "Daisy. Your turn."

I nodded and tried to swallow past the cold dread slithering down my throat. I followed him to a cast iron bench that rested along the edge of Main Street and dropped onto it. The scent of lilacs tickled my nose again, but instead of bringing me joy and peace, they left me nauseous.

Corey sat next to me, and I waited while he pulled out his notebook. To keep him from noticing that my hands shook, I clasped them together and pressed them against the wispy dress that had been my mother's. Then I realized I'd left the potted rosemary back at the table.

When Corey focused his deep green eyes on me, my heart tightened, and it took everything I had not to jump up and run. He studied my face and zeroed in on my eyes. "Are you okay?"

I swallowed and nodded, knowing that I probably looked like the guiltiest person there. "I'm fine."

He arched one brow. "Quite the shock of finding that a fellow witch had been killed deep within the forest."

At least he understood witchy ways. Corey's mom and sister were also of the sisterhood, though they'd moved away from Sweet Mountain Meadows several years ago. I'd thought it funny that Corey had decided to stay. But I was grateful now that I didn't have to explain the intricacies of witchcraft to him in addition to talking about the murder.

"It's truly awful," I managed.

He glanced at his notebook. "I've heard from several others that you were chosen tonight to take Fern's place on the council."

I nodded.

He lifted both brows this time. "Very nice." He shifted on the bench and tilted his head downward closer to mine. "Are you sure you're okay? You might be in shock."

He placed a hand over one of mine, and I nearly came off the bench. "Hey. It's okay. I was just checking to see if your fingers were icy. Could be a sign of shock."

I tightened my cloak about me and shook my head. "No, I'm...it's... I'm fine. I would just like to get this over with so that I can go home."

He nodded. "That's fair. How about we start with an overview of your evening? Tell me who you were with, what you were doing, and anything out of the ordinary that you might have noticed."

I quickly rambled off everything I could remember.

Except when Merry had insulted me.

And meeting Gideon.

And when Merry had interrupted our dance.

So many things I should have told him. I know I should have. But all of them seemed to point to a motivation that I might have wanted Merry dead. I knew I wasn't guilty, but what if the murder weapon *was* my knife?

Goddess help me.

By the time I finished speaking, I was beyond breathless and couldn't help but inhale a large breath of the sweet early summer air.

He studied me so intently that a cold sweat broke out on my forehead. "Did you see Merry this evening? While she was alive, that is."

I nodded. Once again, I had the opportunity to spill my guts, and I didn't.

He wrote in his notebook and glanced back at me. "When and where was the last time you saw her?"

I inhaled a shaky breath. "At the bonfire while I was dancing. Probably around eleven-thirty. It was right before my friends and I headed to Circle."

"What was she doing?" he pressed.

I hesitated for a second, trying to wrangle my thoughts, but it seemed like an eternity passed before I could do so. "She wanted to dance, but her husband wouldn't let her."

That was such a lie. A boulder of angst dropped into my stomach.

Corey nodded and wrote something in his notebook. "Her husband, Carl, correct?"

I widened my eyes. "I don't think she has another one."

He chuckled, making me feel worse. "I'm just checking my facts, ma'am."

Ma'am? He was now calling me ma'am. That had to be a bad sign.

I sat frozen until he addressed me again. "Can you tell me where you were after that, specifically between eleven-forty and midnight?"

I managed another breath and found some relief. I had an alibi. I couldn't be the murderer. I mean, I knew I wasn't, but now Corey would know, too. "After being at the bonfire and dancing, Aeri, Nicole, and I went to the enchanted booth to gather the things we'd left there. Then we walked to Circle together. When we arrived, Jocelyn was there along with Merry's sister, Oriana."

I cringed. Of course, he knew Oriana's relationship to Merry.

He scratched just above his eyebrow. "You three were together the whole time? None of you left each other at any point?"

I nodded and then shook my head. The question he asked was confusing. "We were always together."

Except when I'd danced with Gideon. But my friends were nearby. That had to count.

He jotted in his notebook. Then lifted his gaze and smiled. "I think that's all for now."

I exhaled. "Can I go?"

His smile grew bigger, and I remembered all the times growing up when I'd snuck glances just to watch his beautiful eyes and the interesting expressions on his face. "Sure, you can go. But first, I'd like to offer my congratulations. You received quite an honor tonight."

It sure didn't feel like it. If I'd stayed home, I might have missed out on the fun, might not have been chosen, but I wouldn't be involved in a murder investigation, either. I stood. "Thanks."

Before I could leave, he reached out and caught my arm. "Let me give you my card. In case you think of anything else."

I waited while he pulled a case from his pocket and extracted the card. When he handed it to me, the twinkle in his eyes seemed a tad more than professional, and...seemed to hold some interest in me.

I couldn't fathom the idea, so I snatched his card and hurried off without another word. I should have gone back to the table to get my rosemary and wait for Nicole and Aeri to finish their interviews, but I didn't want to take the chance of encountering Corey again that night.

Instead, I texted my friends, telling them I'd wait for them at the car.

There were enough people around that I wouldn't be isolated, but I needed to be away from the fear and Officer Shelton's discerning gaze and possible flirtations.

TWELVE

The mood in Meowkins Café the next morning was subdued, to say the least. If only it could have been caused by a hangover from drinking too much mead instead of practically witnessing a murder.

I should have stayed home after Nicole dropped me off the night before, but I'd quickly scooped up Freya, and headed to my mom's house instead. A phone call wasn't sufficient to tell her about everything that had happened.

She'd been excited to hear about my appointment, and I'd hated to ruin it by telling her of Merry's death. But if I hadn't, her friends would have surely called first thing as soon as the gossips were up, awake, and able to share the news.

Then my mom had insisted on smudging me, the dress, the cloak, and the house so that any negative energy that might have clung to me would be washed away. After that was all finished, we were both exhausted, and I'd ended up sleeping in her guest bedroom. Although, saying that I'd occupied her guest room might be more correct, because there was little sleeping that had gone on.

At least I had the coffee shop to distract me that morning. We saw our usual early rush of people who stopped in before work, which kept me from talking with my friends much. A bit later, we had a smaller influx of customers as out-of-towners grabbed their morning fix, and then things grew mostly quiet.

I caught Nicole peeking from behind the glass door that separated the café from the Purry Parlor and motioned for her to join Aeri and me. She untied the pink and brown apron she wore and left it on a counter near the door. As she approached, I noticed the same dark circles under her eyes that Aeri and I shared. "Couldn't sleep?" I asked.

She nodded and glanced between the two of us. "You guys, too, I guess."

I released an exhale weighted by everything that had happened the previous day. "Yeah. Hardly any sleep. I think I'll need a double Americano just to get me through the next couple of hours."

Aeri snorted. "I've already had mine, and I'm thinking of a third."

Nicole smiled then. "If you do, you'll be jumpier than an alley cat."

Thank goodness I wasn't going through this alone. I focused on Aeri and asked the question that had burned in my mind since the moment my head had hit the pillow. "Did you mention to Corey that the knife might be mine?"

She quickly shook her head. "No. I don't know for sure that it was."

Nicole released a heavy exhale. "Good. Let's not say anything. For all we know, it fell from your pocket before you reached the festival. Might even be in my car. Let the police do their job. If they discover that it is the murder weapon and question us about it, then we can say something. Otherwise..." She lifted pinched fingers to her lips and twisted them as though turning a lock.

My heart swelled with love for my friends. "I appreciate you guys so much. But please, let's not lie, okay? If they find that it's mine, I'll own that fact. We were all together, so we all have an alibi."

Aeri arched her brow. "Unless they question whether we were all in on it together."

Nicole glanced between us. "No. No way. We don't even have a motive."

Aeri shrugged. "Merry did run you off the road that one time."

I couldn't help but smile. "That was five years ago. No one will even remember it. And Aeri, I'm pretty sure you've never had a run-in with Merry. Even Merry's behavior toward me last night wouldn't be a strong enough motive for murder."

But then why hadn't I mentioned it to Corey?

The lighthearted mood that had just started to appear, vanished like a hunted ground squirrel into its hole.

Aeri exhaled and forced a grin. "So, three Americanos coming up?"

Nicole and I both nodded. Thank the Goddess for caffeine.

We moved to a table near the pastry case so that I could quickly jump up if anyone came in. As we sipped the dark blend that Aeri had crafted perfectly, I gazed at my two friends. "Who do you guys think might have killed her?" I asked it quietly so that the few remaining customers wouldn't overhear.

Nicole set her cup on the table. "Oriana."

There was no doubt in her voice, but some flitted through my mind. "But wouldn't she commit the deed and run off? Why scream and draw attention? Getting caught with the knife in her hand only makes her look guiltier."

Aeri turned to me. "Unless she'd hoped for the reverse effect. An innocent person would stay at the scene of the crime, right? No reason to run off."

Nicole pointed a finger upward. "Oriana might be dumb enough to keep hanging out with her sister, but she's a smart lady otherwise."

I sighed. That was possible. "You know it's expected that I'll visit Oriana now that I'm on the council, to offer my condolences."

"That might be a good thing," Aeri offered.

I rolled my eyes. "I'd rather drink Gilbert's disgusting coffee that Merry tainted."

Aeri shook her head. "No, listen. You'll visit Oriana, and she'll have to let you in *because* you're on the council. What better way to get an opinion of her guilt? You'll have to talk about Merry since that's the reason you're there. It could work out very well."

I took a sip of coffee as I considered her idea and then frowned. "Isn't that the police department's job? To assess guilt?"

Aeri seemed disappointed. "I guess so."

"Besides," I said. "Carl could be the guilty one. He was pretty angry that he had to practically peel Merry away from Gideon when she tried to break up our dance."

Nicole looked upward before she met their gazes again. "Goddess forgive me, but she was a blight upon Sweet Mountain."

I choked on my coffee, almost inhaling it.

Aeri snorted. "A blight? I'd question your harshness, but I'm afraid you're right. Goddess bless her soul."

We all chuckled at that, and our lighthearted mood lasted nearly a minute. Until the door to Meowkins opened, and Sergeant Corey Shelton walked in looking very handsome in his uniform and totally alpha with the gun at his hip.

He visually searched the café until he found me. When he started in our direction, all warmth from the coffee I'd drunk faded into a chill. He reached the table, and with his gaze on me, he lifted his chin. "Daisy? Do you have a moment to talk?"

I swallowed the dread building in my throat and stood. "Of course." I glanced briefly at both my friends, dismayed by the worry and guilt I found there. "Cover the counter for me."

Then I turned to Corey. "No one is in the parlor right now. We can talk there."

He followed me to the glass entrance and opened the door for me. It was a nice gesture, but it didn't make me feel any better. I took a seat on the light brown sofa, and Freya immediately jumped on my lap. I petted her for comfort, and when Corey sat not far from me, I felt a low growl rumble from deep within her.

Corey must have heard her, because he held his palm upward in her direction. "No need to worry about me. I'm just here for a friendly chat."

She hesitated and then sniffed his fingers. I sensed that her wariness of him eased, but not completely. She faced the other cats and lifted her head in what I can only assume was an all-clear.

I stroked her soft gray fur and focused on Corey. "What can I help you with?"

He studied me for a moment, his gaze jumping back and forth between my eyes. Then he exhaled. Any perceived sense of flirtation that might have been there previously was gone. "You didn't tell me the whole truth last night."

I widened my eyes in surprise, which I knew was a big mistake the second after I did. "I...I... How do you mean?"

The beautiful orange tabby that I'd named Friskers jumped on the couch between us, and I was grateful for the distraction.

Corey remained focused on me, and he curved his lips into a smile that said he wasn't buying my innocence. "I learned some interesting things from other witness statements. Several reported that there was a slight altercation between you and Merry while dancing at the bonfire."

Several? I tried to remember who'd been near me, wondering who'd given him my name.

He pulled a notebook from his pocket and flipped the pages. Friskers assumed he was playing and swatted at them. The unmistakable sound of his claw catching paper ripped through the quiet. Corey chuckled and set Friskers on the floor and read from his notebook. "The actual words were 'Merry tried to steal Daisy's date from her while they were dancing'."

He lifted his gaze to me with an expectant look just as Friskers jumped onto the cushion again. Then, my dainty kitty named Angel, with her soft white fur and bright blue eyes, flanked Corey by climbing up the armrest and then continued up to the back of the couch behind the police sergeant where she sniffed him.

I held back a smile.

He absentmindedly rubbed his neck as if she'd bumped him with her nose or tickled him with her whiskers. "If it was a date, then I guess that means you aren't currently married."

My smile flipped into a frown. "No, I'm not." Though I couldn't see how that would come into play anyway. "And Gideon wasn't my date."

Corey nodded and turned to a fresh page in his notebook. One that hadn't been torn. "Gideon?" he repeated. "I don't believe I know him."

I raised a shoulder and let it drop. I hadn't meant to bring him into the conversation, but, well, there he was. "I don't really, either."

Corey glanced up at me. "And?"

"And?" I repeated, not knowing what to say and not wanting to say anything more.

He snorted then and looked at me as if I might be daft. I kind of wondered the same. "What else can you tell me about him?" he asked.

My salt and pepper colored tabby who was barely older than a kitten rubbed against Corey's leg and then attempted to climb his pants. He carefully disengaged Mischief before setting her back on the floor. "You have a lot of cats here."

I released a hollow chuckle. "Sorry. They're not usually this affectionate with strangers."

"If I didn't know better, I'd think they were trying to distract me from our conversation."

Just as he said that, old Grey stood and sauntered in our direction, and I had to wonder if Corey was right.

He glanced at the cats surrounding us. "If that's the case, it's not going to work, kitties. Daisy has to answer my questions."

Unfortunately.

I moistened my dry lips. "I don't know much about Gideon, either. He came into the café yesterday morning. Seemed friendly enough. He must have overheard someone talking about the festival and ended up going."

No, I was not going to mention Merry's appearance that morning or the awful things she'd said to me in front of Gideon. "Or maybe he saw flyers around town, but I saw him there again last night. He asked me to dance, and while we were, a drunken Merry tried to cut in."

"And?" he asked again.

I exhaled, and Freya shifted on my lap. She looked at me, and I could tell she was assessing my emotions. I placed my fingers on her head and stroked down her back to reassure her. "Gideon told Merry no. Then she became...aggressive."

Angel stood on her hind legs, placing her paws on the back of Corey's head, where she continued sniffing. This time, he pulled her from the back of the couch and held her on his lap and petted her. He arched his brow at me. "Aggressive?" he repeated.

I shrugged. "Demanding? Anyway, she didn't want to take no for an answer, but then Carl showed up and dragged her away."

"Dragged?" he clarified.

I smiled then, doing my best to hold onto my patience. "Tugged? I don't know. They left together."

Corey nodded. "Did Carl seem particularly angry with her?"

I snorted. "He wasn't pleased, if that's what you mean."

His gaze hardened. "What I'm asking is if, in your opinion, Carl was angry enough that he might murder his wife."

My blood iced over and stole my snarky attitude. I didn't like talking with Corey about any of it, but he was only doing his job.

I tried to remember those exact moments between Merry and Carl as I pondered his question. "Probably not? He wasn't happy, but he maintained control of himself. He didn't yell at her or get physical. In fact, now that I think of it, he lured her away with the promise of a surprise that he had for her."

Corey set Angel aside and jotted in his notebook as he muttered. "A surprise."

Then he focused on me. "Was that the last you saw of her? No other incidents."

My cheeks heated. "That was it."

He studied me with narrowed eyes for a long moment before he reached into an interior pocket of his jacket. When he pulled out a paper and unfolded it before me, I gasped. It was a photo of a black-handled knife. *My knife.* Dried blood covered the blade, but the peridot gem on the hilt winked at me as though it had no idea that it had partaken in a vicious murder.

THIRTEEN

Corey looked from me to the knife in the picture and back at me. "I take it you recognize this?"

Fear coursed through my veins like ice spiked with barbs. I barely nodded. "It's my athame."

He straightened. "That's what I was told. How about you explain how it became a murder weapon."

I stared at him, beseeching him to believe me. "I don't know. I remember placing it in the pocket of my cloak before I left the house. Then I left my cloak with my items at the enchanted booth with Grover. He stored it there for me until we headed to Circle. When I went to retrieve my knife from my pocket, it was gone."

He scrawled his pen quickly over the page. "That means you could have dropped it at any time, or someone could have taken it from the booth."

I shook my head because neither of those suggestions worked for me. "I guess. Maybe. I mean, I was careful to hold my cloak so that my athame and my chalice wouldn't fall out. They're important to me, and I didn't want to lose them. Also, the enchanted booth is always cast with a spell to keep others from taking what doesn't belong to them, so how could it have been taken from there? Plus, I wore my cloak to Circle, so it couldn't have fallen out then."

He paused for a moment, watching me, as he considered what I'd told him. "Did you check to see that you had your items when you put on your cloak after leaving it at the booth?"

"No," I whispered, angry with myself for not doing so. I should have, but I'd been so caught up in the excitement of feeling pretty and Gideon's attention that my common sense had taken a hike.

He sighed and closed his notebook. "I can't say this looks the best for you, Daisy."

Emotional stress welled behind my eyes. "Am I a suspect then?"

He tapped his pen on his leg. "Not officially. Your alibi clears you of that for now. Unless, of course, we find a reason to believe that Aeri and Nicole covered for you. Or perhaps they went so far as to participate."

I shook my head vehemently. "No, they wouldn't. They didn't. I truly have no idea how or when I lost my knife."

The disappointment in his expression was nothing compared to what I felt myself. "Isn't that a little careless?"

I bit my lip and nodded. "Yes. But the blade's fairly dull. It's not meant to cut anything. Just ceremonial. In order to stab someone to death..." I let my sentence hang as I tried to picture who would be so angry to have enough strength to penetrate Merry's skin with my dull knife.

"A person would need a great deal of force," Corey finished for me.

"I believe so," I said quietly. "They must have been enraged."

He nodded and stood. All the cats except Freya circled around him as though trying to keep him contained.

"Before you go," I said. "Can I ask who recognized my athame?"

He shrugged. "Oriana."

He folded the photo of my knife and placed it inside his jacket pocket. "Thanks for your time, Daisy. You've been helpful."

I inhaled a tentative breath, wondering if I could feel safe. At least for now. "Of course," I said, knowing my reply was totally lame coming from a person who, in fact, had not been the most helpful.

He smiled, and I wondered if he'd thought the same thing. "Do you still have my card?" he asked.

Of course. He'd given it to me less than twelve hours before. Unless he was noting my obvious ability to lose things. I set Freya aside and stood. "Yes."

He nodded with satisfaction and grinned. "Good. Don't forget to call."

With that, he turned toward the door. Mischief dashed in front of him, and he almost tripped trying to avoid her as he made his way out.

I would have chuckled at the antics of the silly kitten, but my thoughts were stuck on what Corey had said. *Don't forget to call?* He'd meant if I remembered anything else, right?

Although he didn't say that. He'd just said to call.

I stared after him, completely confused. One second I'd worried I was a murder suspect. The next, I'd wondered again if he'd been flirting.

Maybe both assumptions were correct.

Or perhaps I'd lost my sanity along with my knife.

Freya meowed, and I picked her up again. "What do you think, baby? Am I in trouble or what?"

She watched me with wide green eyes and then dipped her head in a nod.

I kissed her soft head and placed her on the floor. "I'm afraid you might be right."

With a sigh, I headed back into the main part of the café. Aeri and Nicole now stood behind the counter, as if it was a fortress that might protect them from Corey. As I approached, they looked at me with expectant gazes. "Did he say anything to you guys as he left?" I asked before they could ply me with questions.

Nicole shook her head. "What did he say to you?"

I slumped my shoulders. "Nothing good. Someone told him about the scene with Merry, Gideon, and me while we were dancing. I should have known that wouldn't stay a secret."

Aeri shrugged. "That doesn't prove anything other than Merry was drunk."

I rubbed the third-eye spot between my eyebrows where the beginnings of a headache threatened. "To make matters worse, Corey informed me that, yes, it *was* my knife that had killed Merry. Oriana identified it."

Nicole inhaled sharply. "Oh, no. I'm so sorry, Daisy."

Aeri wrapped an arm about my shoulders and hugged me. "Me, too. But it's going to be okay because you didn't do it."

I looked at her with uncertainty. "We've all heard of innocent people being convicted."

Aeri shook her head. "No, you have a rock-solid alibi, remember?"

Her words didn't ease my fears though. "Yeah, unless the police find something to suggest that you guys covered for me or helped me."

Nicole gasped. "No. That's...no."

Aeri rolled her eyes. "Calm down, ladies. That's even more far-fetched than them pinning this on Daisy alone. One day soon, you'll get your athame back, and we'll send it off with a proper ritual because I'm sure you won't ever want to use it again. Then life will move forward, and we'll put this behind us."

I shuddered at the thought of holding my athame again. "No. Honestly, I don't want it back. Ever. It was a good knife, and it served me well. But even the fires of Hades won't wipe my memory of seeing Oriana holding it over Merry's dead body."

Aeri patted my back. "Of course. Of course." Then she smiled. "We'll search for a new one."

"Yay, shopping!" Nicole piped up with forced cheerfulness. "Count on me for that."

I gave them a half-smile for their efforts to make me feel better. "Actually, Grover gifted Fern's athame to me last night. I never had a chance to tell you. It goes back several generations of witches in my line, and he was certain she'd want me to have it."

Aeri nodded approvingly. "There you go, then. Despite the horrific events, the Goddess has stepped in once again and bestowed luck upon you."

Nicole gave her a genuine smile. "Nice. I can't wait to see it up close."

I nodded but found I didn't want to touch any ritual knives for the time being, so they would have to wait. "There is one thing though. I've decided that having Oriana identify my knife does warrant a visit from me if nothing else. I haven't been to Circle in years, and I can't remember a time where she'd been close enough to me to see the details and now be able to recognize it."

Tiny wrinkles appeared alongside Nicole's eyes as she frowned. "Do you think she, or I guess someone else, purposefully tried to frame you? Personally, I'd imagined Carl had stumbled across it when he was livid with Merry, and he'd committed murder in the heat of the moment."

I studied her warm brown eyes. "I'd like to think her murder wasn't premeditated and that no one was out to frame me, but it feels more personal than that. If someone is trying to hurt me, I need to figure that out sooner than later."

They both nodded solemnly. "Maybe you should visit with Carl, too," Aeri said. "Just to see his reaction. You have a perfectly good reason to go see them both."

I nodded thoughtfully. "Yes, I think I will do just that."

FOURTEEN

I flipped the coffee shop's sign to closed and stepped out the door late that afternoon.

During the busy seasons, I'd stay open later, but for now, I didn't get enough business to cover my expenses. Not to mention, it had been a long day, and I was ready to grab a glass of wine and sink into a deep tub filled with hot water and bubbles.

Warm sunshine cascaded over my shoulders, and as I twisted the key in the lock, the spicy-sweet scent of the purple and lavender stachys growing in the wooden whiskey barrels near my door drifted up and drew a smile from me. The smell would forever remind me of my grandmother. I'd planted these stachys from seeds I gathered each fall, seeds that had originally come from her flowers.

She probably hadn't realized what a gift they'd come to be when she'd given them, but the scent of them always brought happiness.

I pocketed the keys and turned, only to find Gideon striding toward me. He wore a smile, but it didn't extend to his eyes. Part of me warned that I should immediately head off in the opposite direction, but my heart kept me rooted.

He reached out a hand for me as he neared. "Daisy, my lovely. How are you?"

I found myself lifting my hand in return, and he folded it between both of his, surrounding me with warmth. I lifted my gaze to his and searched his expression for any signs of a person who might kill another. "I'm okay. I guess you heard what happened to Merry."

He nodded solemnly. "Yes. I was at the edge of the woods when I heard the scream, and I reached the clearing not long after you all did."

My breaths grew shallow, and fear intertwined with my thoughts. "You were there? Where we found Merry? I didn't see you at all after the ceremony."

He lifted my hand to his lips and pressed a warm kiss on the back of it before he released me. A nice gesture, but I wasn't entirely sure I trusted the man. I folded my arms in front of me so that he couldn't take my hand again.

He followed my movements, and a shadow fell over his face. "You're wondering why I didn't come forward."

He'd read my thoughts so well. "Yes, actually. The police interviewed the rest of us, but I guess not you. Unless you talked to them later."

He quickly shook his head. "I would have come forward if I'd had anything to add, but there's nothing I could have said that would help with their investigation."

That explanation didn't sit right with me. "I'm sure there were plenty of people that they questioned who didn't have anything to add. But still, that's the police's job to determine, isn't it? Not ours. Many times, people have seen something they didn't think was valuable, but when put together with the other pieces of the puzzle, it ended up helping the authorities."

He inhaled a deep breath and released it slowly, carefully watching me as he did. "This is truly unfortunate."

I looked at him with bewilderment. "What's unfortunate? Me asking questions? Or you hiding in the shadows?"

Understanding flickered in his eyes, and he gave me a solemn smile. "No. What's unfortunate is that the passing of Merry has created unnecessary contention between us."

I didn't feel it was unnecessary at all. If he was a murderer, I'd like to know before I allowed him to flirt with me again. "I would disagree. It seems to me, Mr. McKay, that you might be hiding something."

He blinked slowly and shook his head. "It's not what you think, my lovely. I did not kill Merry."

I narrowed my gaze. "Is that what you think I'm thinking?" I mean, it was, but he was presumptuous.

Unless he could read my thoughts. Which he might. Though he'd said he could read me while we'd been at the festival, by which he could have meant body language. But still.

He glanced down the street before he turned back to me. "If you will permit me to buy you dinner, I will explain."

Did I want to eat with him? I wasn't sure. Though I did want an answer that I could judge to see if his excuse was credible. If we were in a public place, I'd be safe, plus he had been very kind to me. Maybe he didn't deserve my mistrust.

Perhaps, I should go. Unless, he'd used me as a distraction, a reason to be in the vicinity so that he'd have had access to Merry. He'd told me they were business partners, but that didn't mean they'd gotten along well or that things were what he'd like them to be.

Goddess help my poor confused mind. "Fine. I'll agree on one condition. I'd like you to tell me exactly what kind of business dealings you had with Merry. And what your true relationship to her was. Because I think there's more to that than you're saying."

He chuckled and dipped his head. "As you wish. Though that was my intent all along. There are indeed things about me that you should know."

An unexpected shiver radiated outward from my core. "Then we should eat somewhere here, along Main Street. Somewhere in public where we can walk to."

He grinned, and unwanted attraction tugged on my heart. "Absolutely, my lovely. I was thinking of Deliziosa."

I turned in the direction where he'd looked only moments before. Perhaps he wasn't intending to cart me off and murder me after all. "Deliziosa is acceptable."

Gideon offered his arm to me, but I responded with a small shake of my head. "There are things I need to know about you before I allow you to get any closer to me."

He dipped his head in understanding. "Of course. At least we have a common goal."

I was afraid to ask what that goal might be.

He opened his hand wide and swept it to the side. "I'll let you lead the way."

We walked the block and a half together in silence. I took the opportunity to assess any negative vibes that might be coming from his direction, but I was unable to read him like he'd done with me. Which, for some reason, drove me utterly insane. There was more to him. I knew it.

The second Gideon opened the door for me to Deliziosa, the scent of roasted garlic and baking bread ignited my tastebuds, but I kept my reaction to myself. In addition to the linguini that my mom and I loved, the chicken parmigiana was fantastic, along with their Merlot.

The hostess led us to a quiet table near the front of the restaurant, and I did allow Gideon to help me with my chair. The man was a gentleman, but there was nothing that said dangerous people couldn't be handsome with good manners, up until they did the unthinkable deed.

Gideon opened his menu and then met my gaze. "The house Merlot here is quite nice."

I stared into his clear blue eyes and wondered once again if he was reading my thoughts. "Yes. It's my preferred choice as well."

His smile widened into something spectacular. "It seems we both have impeccable taste."

I tried not to smile in return but failed. "It seems so. That, or you're an expert in mindreading."

Merriment danced in his eyes. "As much as that would be of value, especially where you're concerned, I must admit that I don't possess that particular skill."

I was about to ask him which skills he did possess, but our server, a young man with bright orange hair, who I knew was Mona's grandson, appeared with glasses of ice water and a delightful bread basket full of warm, crusty bread sticks. He took our order and left. A few minutes later, he returned and poured us each a glassful of dark red wine.

When we were alone again, I lifted my glass, pondering where I should start with my interrogation.

He raised his as well. "To new friends and future possibilities."

I drank to his possibilities and set my glass in front of me.

He smiled. "I can see you have many questions."

I focused my gaze intently on him and nodded. "I do. The first thing I would like to know is why you're here in Sweet Mountain Meadows. Yes, you had business dealings with Merry, but what exactly were they? For as long as I knew her, she didn't bother with earning money. Only spending it. Carl handled all their financial affairs."

Gideon chuckled, the sound deep and rich, and full of amusement. "I should have known you'd get straight to the core of the issue."

I wasn't sure exactly what that issue was, but I didn't mind the compliment. Maybe I was savvier than I'd realized. "Yes, please expound on that."

What I swore was worry darkened his demeanor, and he suddenly seemed less sure of himself. He took a sip of wine and then met my gaze. "I suppose there's no beating around the bush with this one. I find that I like you, Daisy. I can't say specifically what drew me to you, but you intrigue me. I enjoy your company very much. This is not something I can say has happened to me before during my nearly four and a half decades on Earth."

Wait. *What?*

I replayed his words in my mind and then snorted. "You are *not* in your mid-forties. I just turned forty, and you're younger than me."

By far, if I wanted to be honest.

He smiled, but I sensed something akin to impending doom in his emotions. "It may seem so, but the kind of blood flowing through my veins doesn't age as fast as most."

He wasn't a witch then. A vampire, perhaps. Though they aged quite a bit slower than humans, and my friends and I had already decided that his skin wasn't pale enough. Werewolf? I didn't have any experience in that realm, so I really couldn't say.

His worried emotions became mine, and my stomach muscles tightened in response. "What kind of blood, then?" I asked quietly.

Gideon reached over and took my hand. I should have pulled away, but his intense gaze kept me rooted in place. He leaned close, though there weren't others nearby that might hear him. "I am a demon."

FIFTEEN

I stared at Gideon, wondering if I possibly could have misunderstood his declaration. "Excuse me?"

Gideon nodded as if to assure me that he'd spoken the truth. He was, in fact, a demon.

My difficulties didn't come from not hearing him. Or not knowing what a demon was. I thought I did. At least for the most part. But my mind refused to connect the two, to believe that the handsome man sitting before me with uncertainty written all over his face was, in fact, a dark entity.

Yes, I'd sensed a darkness before, but not *that* kind.

It took several moments before my better senses finally kicked in. He wasn't serious. No. He'd been teasing me. Making fun of what he would consider my unfounded fear of him. The joke was on me.

I snorted. "Dear Goddess, you almost had me believing that one."

Gideon gave me a gentle smile and squeezed my hand. He held my gaze for several moments, and then his lovely blue eyes darkened into obsidian. The sight was such a shock that I inhaled sharply, causing me to choke.

The color of his eyes returned to normal as he removed his hand from mine. He lifted my water glass and held it out to me. I swallowed, calming the suffocating feeling, but then I kept swallowing and swallowing, knowing that as long as I did, he couldn't expect me to speak.

It was a brief but much needed reprieve.

When the glass was empty, I set it carefully on the table in front of me. Slowly, I lifted my gaze to him.

He arched a questioning brow, waiting for a response from me.

The only problem was that I didn't have one. I held out for several uncomfortable seconds and then spoke. "I don't know what to say to that."

He started to speak, but then our server arrived with dinner and placed our plates before us. "Everything look okay?"

Gideon turned his gaze upward to the young man, and I swear his eyes darkened again. "It looks delicious. Thank you. And now, we require some private time. I'll signal you when you're needed again."

A deep blush colored the poor kid's cheeks. "Yes, sir." With that, he hurried away.

Instead of lifting his fork, Gideon focused on me. "I don't ask that you say much, Daisy. I would just like to know if you're comfortable being in my presence now that you know what I am."

A million thoughts raced through my mind but feeling scared wasn't one of them. Maybe it should have been. Still, he was the same Gideon that he'd been a few minutes before. The same charming man who'd flirted and danced with me at the Beltane Festival.

But, of course, I'd been in the dark about him, then, so I hadn't been looking for warning signs. I wondered if it would be careless on my part to continue to talk to him? Dangerous even?

When I finally responded, I said the only thing that I could formulate into decent words. "I'm not afraid of you, if that's what you're asking."

He relaxed against his chair and offered me a relieved smile. "Thank you, Daisy. You are a warm and gracious person."

His reaction surprised me. He'd been nervous that I'd reject him. Somehow, that knowledge, that vulnerability, eased the remainder of doubts that I had. "Do you typically receive a bad response when you tell people?"

I imagined he might.

He shrugged and lifted his fork. "Perhaps. Normally, I don't reveal my identity to anyone but those I hold close to my heart. And of course, those who've requested my services."

His services. Wow. I didn't want to think about those right now.

Instead, I lifted my fork and knife and sliced off a piece of chicken. "Then why did you feel compelled to tell me?"

He sipped his wine. "I told you that I like you, and I suppose that I needed to know if you could accept me as I am."

I wondered if I could as well. "Tell me truthfully, then. Did you have anything to do with Merry's death?"

I wasn't sure if he'd be honest or not, but if he lied, perhaps I could catch a telltale sign.

He held my gaze and shook his head. "No. I had nothing to do with her demise."

His answer seemed genuine, but then a harsh realization hit. "Oh, my Goddess. You might not have killed her, but you took her soul, didn't you?"

Black flashed in his eyes, but he didn't look away from me. "I did."

Things were starting to make more sense now. "Was that the business you had with Merry? You'd come here to collect?"

"Not exactly. Yes, she'd desired to sell her soul. I drove down from Oregon, brokered the deal, but it might have been years before it was time for me to retrieve it."

I stared over the rim of my glass of wine as I took a drink and tried to piece together what I'd learned. "You don't take souls immediately after a deal?" I asked.

He finally sliced into his chicken. "What would be the point then? A person would reap no benefit from the agreement."

I suppose that made sense. "So, they receive a limited amount of time before you come back?"

He shrugged. "The amount of time depends on the contract."

"What about Merry?"

He chuckled then. "I'm not at liberty to discuss the details, but I can say that she had a while."

"Then why did she die?"

"Ah, Daisy, my lovely. That is the question, isn't it?"

It was indeed. I tried a different tactic. "Do you know who murdered her?"

He finished chewing before he answered. "No. I know nothing of the details of her death, other than the notification I received when her body neared the expulsion of her soul."

"That's an interesting way to explain death."

He shrugged. "It's accurate. When a body dies, the soul is forced out because of inhabitable living conditions."

I twirled spaghetti on my fork and ate as I pondered what I'd just learned. "You receive notifications? How does that work? A text message or something?"

A twinkle landed in his eyes. "A text message? Funny. No, I would describe it more as a knowing."

"A knowing?"

"Yes. In my soul."

That was a surprise. "You have a soul?"

He placed a hand over his heart as though I'd wounded him. "Of course, I do. I could also choose to barter it away like others if I wanted."

I tilted my head, intrigued by the complexity of my dinner partner. "But you won't."

"No. Let's just say I've witnessed the implications of such a deal. I prefer to live a natural life, to enjoy the good that comes my way, like meeting you, and work through the difficult times."

Something that flickered in his eyes spoke of those difficult times, but asking about them now seemed inappropriate. "I thought I felt Merry's soul at the crime scene. Is she still around?"

I couldn't believe I was at dinner discussing a dead person's soul, while casually eating chicken parmigiana.

He shook his head. "Her soul was dispatched within moments."

"And yet you're still in town."

He smiled. "Yes."

This was one question I needed the answer to. "Why?"

He studied me for a long moment. "Let's just say I have a vested interest in seeing the person who committed the crime brought to justice."

I'd been certain he was going to say he wanted to see more of me, and it stung that he hadn't. "Are you waiting so that you can collect the murderer's soul, too?"

He hesitated and then shook his head. "No. Something went awry, Daisy."

I frowned. "How do you mean?"

He sighed. "Again, I can't disclose details, but typically, a person who's signed away her soul can't die within days."

"Merry was protected?"

His eyes sparkled with mischief, and I knew he wouldn't or couldn't answer that question. Instead, he lifted his wineglass and drank.

When he set it down, he met my gaze and gave me a warm smile. "I should be honest here, as well, Daisy. I have another motivation, which is to ensure that you are not held accountable for another's actions before I leave town."

My heart might have fluttered at that. "I appreciate that, Gideon, though I don't see how I could be charged with her murder. I admit it worries me, but when I look at things realistically, I think I'll be okay. I do have a solid alibi."

He gave a quick nod. "Still."

I bit into a bread stick and decided to tell him the plans I'd concocted with Aeri and Nicole earlier in the day. "I've actually considered looking into things on my own. I'd rather be proactive than play the victim."

He nodded in approval. "I think that's a great idea."

My gaze jumped to his. "Really? You're serious?"

"Very. A person can accomplish a lot if she puts her mind to it. And, as I've learned from my nephew's girlfriend, an average person can sometimes gain access to information that the police can't get without a warrant. Or things they might not ever get because some people are unwilling to talk to them."

Hearing that intrigued me. "Your nephew's girlfriend? She sleuths on her own?"

He nodded. "She also happens to be a witch. You know, Daisy, I would be more than happy to assist you, too. I can't become too deeply involved. You understand. But there are ways I can help."

Before I could respond and accept his offer, he jerked his gaze upward and looked beyond my shoulder. A fraction of a second later, I sensed someone close by and turned my head to investigate.

Corey, complete with uniform and gun, was headed straight for us, and there was no time for me to crawl under the table and hide.

SIXTEEN

The expressions on Gideon's and Corey's faces were guarded as Corey approached our table with one hand resting on the butt of his gun and the other holding a takeout bag from Deliziosa. Gideon flicked his gaze to me and murmured, "Fear not, Daisy."

I wasn't sure if he meant I had nothing to worry about because nothing would happen, or if he meant he could protect me if it came to that. But *that* was exactly what I did worry about.

I'd never had two men...doing whatever they were doing because of me, and I didn't want it now.

Corey reached our table and gave me a brief nod. "Evening, Daisy."

I followed with a quick smile. "Good evening, Corey. Is everything all right?"

He shot a suspicious look at Gideon before he looked back at me. "I was going to ask you the same."

I drew my brows together in confusion. "Yes, of course. We're just having dinner."

Corey turned to Gideon. "I don't believe we've met."

Gideon stood and held out a hand. "Gideon McKay at your service."

Corey hesitated and then shook it. "Sergeant Corey Thompson. I'm leading the investigation of the Mercer Murder case. I've been trying to locate you, Mr. McKay, but you never seem to be in your hotel room."

He shrugged and glanced about. "Why would I want to stay cooped up in my room when I have this beautiful town to explore? Is there something I can assist you with?"

Corey puffed out his chest. "I'd like you to come to the station and give me a formal statement of any details you can remember from last night concerning Merry Mercer."

Gideon lifted his chin in acknowledgement. "I'd be happy, too."

Corey remained rooted where he was, staring at Gideon.

A look of surprise flashed across Gideon's face. "What? You mean right now?"

Corey held his gaze. "If it's not inconvenient."

He couldn't be serious. Gideon started to speak, but I held up my hand and stood. "Let me."

I turned to Corey. "Can we take this outside?"

People were starting to stare, and I wasn't about to let him ruin my evening.

He glanced between Gideon and me and then nodded. Apparently, as long as I was with him, he wasn't concerned about my dinner companion.

I gripped his elbow and tugged him from the restaurant.

Outside, a cool breeze slid down the canyon and swirled around us. With the sun now behind the mountains, the temperature was dropping quickly. I paused not far from the door and glared up at Corey. "What is this all about? Why are you interrupting our dinner?"

He seemed surprised by my answer. "I was concerned for you. This Gideon McKay is an unknown entity, and I've been trying unsuccessfully to contact him. To be honest, I'm not sure what he's capable of."

I snorted. "I can appreciate that. But did I look like I was under duress, eating in a public restaurant?"

He shrugged one shoulder. "That's not always easy to discern. I'll be honest, Daisy. I don't like the guy. There's something fishy about him."

And I knew exactly what. "We're just having dinner."

He stared down at me and arched his brow. "A date then? Last night wasn't, but today is?"

My patience was wearing thin. "As I said, last night was *not* a date. I went to the festival with my friends. Gideon happened to be there. Tonight is just dinner. He had something he wanted to discuss with me."

Corey narrowed his eyes. "What would that be?"

I hated to say it, but it had become clear that I needed to delineate a boundary. "A personal matter."

He seemed taken aback by my reply.

"Look, Corey. I appreciate your concern, and I understand that you need to talk to everyone who had contact with Merry. But I'm not in any danger right now, and I don't believe Gideon is a dangerous man." To most people anyway. "I don't intend to go off anywhere alone with him, and Gideon's willing to give you a statement. There's no emergency here."

He exhaled and shifted his stance. The proper thing to do would be to let me get back to my evening, but he didn't seem inclined to do that. "I actually wanted to talk to you about something, too."

I widened my eyes. "Okay. What is it?"

"We've located Oriana's ring."

My breath whooshed out of me. That was not the news I'd expected since I didn't know Oriana had involved the police, but I'd take it. "That's great. Where was it?"

He lifted a sardonic brow. "It was in Merry's purse."

I blinked in surprise. "Are you kidding me? That...*woman*," I said with more ire than I should have. "Merry had been with Oriana when she'd accused me of stealing it. And she'd had it the whole time."

If Merry wasn't dead, I'd have a thing or two to say to her. "Too bad you can't question her about it. Or even prosecute her for theft."

He chuckled. "I think it has more sentimental value than anything. I doubt a judge would hear the case."

Some of the weight I hadn't realized I was carrying faded. "Still. She owes me an apology that I'll never get."

He gazed at me with discerning eyes. "Does that make you angry?"

I scoffed. "Not angry enough to kill her, if that's what you're asking. Besides, I didn't know Merry had taken the ring until just now."

He lifted his chin. "Good point."

"Also," he continued. "We haven't been able to prove that Merry stole it. We may never be able to. It's also possible that someone could have planted it there to make Oriana look guilty of murder."

My instincts fired a warning. I'd better keep any future thoughts about Merry or Oriana to myself, or I might end up looking more guilty. "Thank you for letting me know. It's a relief."

He glanced toward the restaurant and then back at me.

"Was there something else?" I asked.

He hesitated a moment before he spoke. "I guess that's it. I'll let you get back to dinner. Just be careful, Daisy. Your new position comes with power, you know, and there are those who might exploit that."

I wasn't sure exactly which powers he referred to other than that I would have input on the direction of the coven. And I wasn't sure why he'd think Gideon would exploit them since he'd shown interest in me before I'd been chosen. Even still, I knew Corey was only looking out for me. "Thank you."

He lifted his brow. "You still have my card?"

I reassured him with a nod. It had only been a day since he'd given it to me. Only hours since he'd asked the last time. "Yes, I sure do."

He smiled. "Okay. Call me."

His repeated suggestion left me baffled. "I will. Have a good night." I strode back into the restaurant before he could waylay me again.

Gideon stood as I approached the table. "Everything okay?"

I released a weighted exhale and resumed my seat. "I think so."

Though I wouldn't bet my life on it.

He didn't seem convinced. "What was his problem?"

I sighed. "He's concerned about me because you're an outsider, but I let him know everything is okay."

He narrowed his gaze. "Does he have a reason to be possessive of you? Boyfriend? Past lover?"

I snorted a soft laugh. "No. Not at all. Also, Corey wanted to tell me that they've located Oriana's stolen ring. Merry had it in her purse."

Gideon opened his thumb and finger into a V and stroked his chin. "That's curious, isn't it?"

I raised my brows to show my interest in the information. Though I wasn't buying into the idea of someone planting the ring to make Oriana look guilty, because Merry was the exact kind of person who would steal from her sister. "Yes, very interesting. I would imagine that Oriana wasn't too happy to learn that. Merry certainly made her look like a fool, bringing her to the café and encouraging her to accuse me of taking it when Merry knew where it was the whole time."

He lifted his glass and swirled the remainder of his wine. Then he focused on me. "Unless someone planted it in Merry's purse after the murder."

"Corey said the same thing."

Gideon frowned at the comparison. "I suppose the sergeant is somewhat competent then. Even so, Oriana must be their number one suspect, don't you think?"

Our conclusions were the same. "It seems that way to me."

He studied me. "Do you intend to speak with Oriana during your investigations?"

"Oh, yes. I would very much like a chance to read her when I ask about Merry and the ring."

He nodded. "Good. That sounds like a solid plan. If you're agreeable, I'd like to discuss what you learn from her."

I found that I very much would like the same. "That would be helpful."

I opened the contacts app on my phone and typed in his name. Feeling brave and bold, I handed it to him. "I'm going to need your number."

SEVENTEEN

The next day, after the morning rush of customers, I left Aeri in charge and climbed into my old but dependable Toyota. Oriana and her husband Bill lived at the bottom of the road that climbed the mountain and led to the ski slopes above, as well as Merry's beautiful home snuggled amidst the evergreen pines and beautiful aspens, whose leaves danced in the breeze.

I parked alongside the road in front of Oriana's older red brick home. Her car was in the drive, and thankfully, Bill's wasn't. As far as I was concerned, he was a male clone of Merry. Perhaps Oriana had subconsciously picked him because it was a personality type that she was accustomed to, even if it was an undesirable one.

Bright Pink tulips and purple pansies thrived along the front of Oriana's house, and I'd heard she was an expert garden witch. Merry probably hated that because she hadn't excelled at anything in particular.

Not that I had either. I could brew an excellent cup of coffee, but a coffee witch wasn't exactly a thing. Though my baking skills had improved through the years, and I did have a way with animals.

I rang the bell and waited. And waited. And waited. And then gave up. I was certain I was in the presence of another witch, but I couldn't force her to open the door if she didn't want to talk to me.

So much for my first attempt at sleuthing. I couldn't even make contact with my target. Perhaps I needed to regroup and come up with a better plan.

As I headed back to my car, I caught sight of Katelyn power-walking up the opposite side of the street, headed away from me, her short brown hair pulled back into a ponytail that stuck straight out. I wasn't sure if she'd have any useful information, but it couldn't hurt to ask.

Plus, she'd also been in line for succession, along with the rest of us, which made her a suspect if I was. Though her motive to kill Merry might be considered less than mine, I wondered if Corey had looked closely at her as well.

I hurried across the quiet street and called her name as I approached.

Katelyn slowed, glanced over her shoulder, and then stopped. "Oh, hi, Daisy. What are you doing out here this morning?"

I thumbed over my shoulder. "I thought I should pay my respects to Oriana. I know we're not the best of friends, but since I'm now…"

The rest of my words felt awkward on my tongue, and I let them fade away.

Katelyn nodded knowingly. "The newest member of the council," she finished for me. "Do you mind if we keep walking? I need to get my steps in before work."

I shook my head, and she resumed her pace, with me working to keep up alongside her. "Unfortunately, Oriana's not at home."

"She's probably at the funeral home or something," Katelyn supplied, and she was likely correct.

I filled my lungs, trying to compensate for my exertion. "Seeing her over Merry's body like that was…"

"Tragic," Katelyn finished. "Truly it was. I haven't seen Oriana since, but I'm sure she's a wreck."

I slid a sideways glance in Katelyn's direction. "You don't think she could have killed her though, do you?" It was as good of a conversation starter as any.

Katelyn wrinkled her nose. "It's hard to fathom that she could, though when people commit horrific crimes, those around them often seem truly shocked."

She had a point. "Honestly, unless it's some random stranger, then her murderer could be one of us."

Katelyn eyed me carefully. "Speaking of strangers, I'd wondered about that Gideon guy that you were with. Handsome, though he has to be, what, ten years younger than you?"

Her possible insinuation that I was with a man who was out of my league caught me off guard and left me without words.

Which didn't matter because she kept right on speaking. "He did publicly embarrass Merry when he refused to dance with her. Perhaps, he stole your athame while he was leading you around the dance floor."

I was shocked to learn that might be what she and others were thinking. "No. My knife was with Grover at that time, protected in the enchanted booth and hidden in my cloak. Gideon couldn't have had access to it. Besides, I'm sure Grover would have mentioned it if an outsider had stepped inside our booth."

She nodded thoughtfully. "Hmm..."

I don't know why I felt the need to defend Gideon. He seemed quite capable of taking care of himself. But I did. "Honestly, I'd wondered about Gideon for a moment or two as well, but I've talked to him since, and there's really no reason he'd kill her. If Merry had approached him again later last night, he would have extricated himself like he had the first time."

My nearly breathless attempts to persuade her only partially worked, and suspicion still lingered in her eyes. "If not him," Katelyn said. "Then my next guess would be Carl."

We disagreed on that. "Not Oriana?"

Katelyn shook her head. "I know Merry was often mean to Oriana, but they were sisters, and Oriana could have walked away at any point. Not so with Carl. He would need a divorce, and you know as well as I do that Merry would have taken him for every cent a lawyer could get."

That was a definite strike against Carl.

"Not that they had that much money left for Merry to take," she added.

She had my attention now. "What do you mean? I thought Carl made a lot of money. At least, Merry had always claimed he did."

Katelyn snorted. "He does, but Merry had no problem spending it as fast as he brought it in and then some. She had as much control over her spending as she did her drinking."

I snorted. Merry might have been able to hide her money issues but not her drinking problem, both of which would have contributed to marital problems.

I'd gotten enough information to know where I was headed next. "Thanks for the chat, Katelyn, but my thighs say I've had enough for today."

She grinned. "Aw, come on. It's good for you. If you're going to keep up with that younger man, you'd best be in shape."

I chuckled and considered hexing her with chin hairs. "Yes, but it won't be good for you if I pass out on the sidewalk. I'll catch up with you later."

She lifted a hand as she headed off. "Sounds good."

I paused to catch my breath and to check how far it was back to my car. We'd covered a fair distance, but at least the way back was downhill. Driving to Carl and Merry's home would give me sufficient time to recover.

I hoped.

Halfway up the mountain, I spotted Merry and Carl's mailbox and turned into their driveway. Instead of a massive Alpine chalet, as Merry had liked to brag about, I found a modest home, still pretty though, with a wood and stone exterior hidden away amongst pines and aspens. Carl had left the garage open, and I spotted Merry's black SUV and Carl's white truck parked inside.

Their place was higher than most in Sweet Mountain Meadows, and Merry's red tulips and purple grape hyacinth still had fresh blooms. It hit me very suddenly that Merry, as awful as she could be, would never again look upon her flowers or sleep in her bed as a full-blooded human. Even though Merry probably didn't deserve my sympathy, it still left me sad. If she hadn't been dispatched to wherever Gideon had sent her, she might have lingered here as a ghost.

I knocked on the door, and this time, I was lucky enough to have Carl answer. He peeked out from the darkened interior, with equally dark shadows coloring the bags under his bloodshot eyes, and a layer of brown stubble flecked with gray covered his square jawline. He looked like death warmed over, but at least he was still willing to communicate with the outside.

He attempted a smile and failed. "Daisy," he said, and I could sense him questioning why I was there.

It was true that I didn't get out in the community that often, but I wasn't a complete hermit. "Hi, Carl. I just wanted to drop in and see if there's anything I can do for you."

He drew his fingers back across his unruly hair. "I don't think so."

Now that I'd satisfied his curiosity about why I was there, he didn't seem as interested in speaking to me. I was about to flop at my second attempt to investigate, and I searched frantically for a reason to keep him talking. "It's important to have friends and family around you at this time."

He lifted his chin in acknowledgement. "Yeah, thanks."

Carl started to shut the door, but I raised my hand to stop him, frantically searching for a way to keep him talking. "I was wondering if you've sensed Merry's ghost about the house? That might bring you some comfort."

He widened his eyes in alarm. "What?"

I shrugged. "You know, when someone is murdered, their spirit tends to stick around, to haunt the places where they'd lived or died. Or just to stay for a bit with family."

He dropped his face into his hand. "Please, God, no," he muttered, making me wonder which emotion caused him to say such a thing. Was he concerned with her possible unrest for her sake or because he feared he'd never be rid of her?

Guilt from causing him further distress nipped at me. But I wasn't making it up. Murdered people did sometimes linger long after they separated from their bodies. Though I did know Merry was no longer around.

"I thought I could offer my services. On behalf of the council, you know? I could check to see if she's still here if you'd like. If I sense anything, I could do a smudge to help her along if that's your preference."

His resistance faded, and he stepped back to allow me to enter. "Uh, okay. Sure. That might be a good idea."

I glanced about the entryway and upward to the high ceiling and the chandelier that hung from a wooden beam. "Have you sensed her at all?"

He shook his head. "But I'll be honest with you. I spent most of yesterday hiding in a bottle and have the killer headache today to prove it. Merry used to make me a concoction that helped, but..."

He widened his empty hands, drawing sympathy from me. "I'm so sorry. Yes, I believe I know the potion that you're talking about. It's been in our family for generations. If you'd like, and if you don't mind me being about your kitchen poking into things for ingredients, I could make it for you."

Carl rubbed a hand over his bleary eyes. "Could you? That would be great. I need to start planning her funeral, but I can barely think."

I did realize, of course, that people grieved in different ways. But he had yet to shed a tear or talk about how he couldn't live without her. "Sure. Show me the way to your kitchen. You can keep me company while I brew."

And, of course, question him. Without appearing to do so, which reminded me to tread lightly on topics of interest.

The kitchen was just as gorgeous as the rest of the house despite the pile of dirty dishes in the sink. I had to hand it to Merry. She did know how to decorate. Though a decorating witch wasn't any more of a thing than a coffee witch.

Carl hitched up his plaid green flannel pants before he planted himself on a stool next to a large gray countertop.

He looked like he could use a good meal. "I can make you something to eat," I offered.

"Nah. If you take care of the headache, I can manage myself."

I nodded. "Sure."

I found the entryway to the pantry at the far end of the kitchen. "Does she keep everything in here?"

"Did," he responded, reminding me that she would no longer be brewing potions, either.

I stepped inside and found shelves of food storage, large pots and pans, along with various small kitchen appliances. The shelves behind me held a witch's paradise. I glanced across a multitude of jars full of crushed flowers, herbs, leaves, and stems of every plant I'd ever used to craft potions or use for rituals. She even had fragments of bone, which I knew were only used for dark magic, which also didn't surprise me one bit.

The jars all matched, and they'd been marked with cute, decorative labels. It was so unlike the mishmash of whatever I currently had in my cupboards, and I vowed to do a better job of organizing.

I quickly selected the herbs I'd need, placed them in a small cauldron that would fit on a stove, and returned to the main part of the kitchen. Carl sat with his head down, resting it on his folded arms on the counter. "This shouldn't take too long," I said.

"Thanks," he mumbled.

I'd made this concoction so many times in my life that I knew the exact recipe. I boiled water, added herbs, and whispered the words that would infuse the required energy into my brew.

When I finished, I used a ladle to partially fill a coffee cup that I'd found in a nearby cupboard. I added a little milk and sugar to make it more palatable, and placed the mug in front of Carl. "Here you go."

He lifted his head, then the mug, and sniffed. "Smells right." He took a small sip and exhaled his relief.

I smiled, liking that I could use my powers for good. "Shouldn't take long to start working."

He nodded. "Yeah. I know."

Of course, he did. Merry had likely made it for him many times. "I think I'll wait until it's kicked in before I check the house for Merry's ghost. Then you can show me around, and I won't miss any places."

He took another long drink. "Her smudge stuff is in the pantry, too. Look for a clear box with a purple lid."

I did as he suggested and pulled out a small bundle of white sage. It would help with negative energy all around. I found a dark blue ceramic plate on the shelf next to the box and figured she probably used that to catch any ash as she walked.

When I returned, Carl was already looking much better. "Matches?" I asked, knowing that my fire creating skills could also use some work.

He retrieved them for me, and I lit the sage, allowing the dried leaves and stems to begin to smolder. I positioned myself on the opposite side of the counter. "I'll just let that burn for a bit in this room. Kitchens tend to have strong energy, especially if Merry had cast spells here."

He straightened a little and stared at me, leaving me uncomfortable with the silence. Now seemed like as good of a time as any to casually start the conversation.

"What do you remember about that night, Carl? I know Merry never made it to Circle. When did you last see her?"

He exhaled a weighted breath and shook his head. "The last time I saw her was not long after the last time you did."

I tilted my head. "How do you mean?"

He sniffed, but he wasn't teary-eyed. "When I pried her away from that guy you were dancing with."

Lured might have been more accurate. "I remember you'd said you had a surprise for her, which made her go with you willingly. What was it?"

He rolled his eyes and snorted. "I didn't have anything, but I knew she'd follow me if I said that. She was making a damn spectacle of herself."

"And embarrassing you," I added.

"Yeah," he said as he released a forceful breath. Then he met my gaze. "You have *no* idea what it was like to live with her, Daisy. Nagging day in and day out. Never happy with anything I gave her. Always wanting more, more, more."

I nodded, encouraging him to continue. "She could be a hard person to be around."

He snorted. "And you saw her, what, a few times a year? Try living with her. I should be sad that she's gone, but I'm not, Daisy. I'm just not."

I swallowed and casually patted my pocket to make sure my phone and magic-infused pepper spray were there in case he suddenly regretted his confession. "You sound like there was no love lost when she passed."

"There wasn't," he said bluntly.

I wanted to ask, but I was afraid. Still, I knew I had to, or I'd be disappointed in myself. "You didn't kill her, Carl, did you?"

He glanced down, away from my scrutiny, and shook his head. "No. I didn't kill her."

I dug deep for more bravery. "What *did* you do after she left with you?"

Carl looked up then. "I tried to get her to go home with me, but when she realized there was no surprise, she was angry. She insisted on going back to the festival. I tried to force her into the car, and she punched me. I think she was trying to hit my face, but she only managed to get me here."

He tugged on the collar of his shirt and revealed a purple and red mark at the base of his neck about the size of my knuckles. "After that, I let her go. I'd had enough. I prayed to the Goddess that she wouldn't be chosen as Fern's successor, because that would only turn her into more of a monster, and then I went home. I crashed until about two in the morning when the police knocked on my door."

He did choke up on his last words, but there were still no tears in his eyes.

But I sure felt a knot of emotion in my guts. "I'm so sorry, Carl. I know you were good to her. Better than she deserved."

Though I wasn't convinced of his innocence. "I should probably start that smudge and head out before too long. I told my mom I was stopping here first, but she'll be expecting me."

That was a lie. I hadn't talked to my mom at all that day. But I'd hoped if he thought someone knew where I was, it would be a deterrent to him if he realized he'd said too much and felt the need to dispatch me, too.

That was, if he'd murdered his wife in the first place. He could have hated his life with Merry, but that didn't mean he'd killed her.

Carl showed me each room, and I smudged as quickly as I could, getting smoke above and below and into each of the corners. When we finished, we returned to the kitchen, and I crushed the tip of the sage until it no longer smoldered. "That should help dispel any negative energy, and luckily, I sensed no sign of Merry here to bother you."

"Thank God and the Goddess for that."

He walked me to the front door, and I turned to him before I left. "I made extra of that potion. Its power is already waning, but it should last another day or so, even if it's not as strong."

He nodded. "Thank you, Daisy. I'm glad you stopped by."

I found that I could genuinely smile at him. "I'm glad I did, too. Please call if you need anything else."

With that, I left and hurried to my car. Only once I was inside with the doors locked and backing out of the driveway did I feel like I could truly breathe again.

EIGHTEEN

When I reached the bottom of the mountain road, I pulled off to the side and parked. I knew that I shouldn't trust Gideon a hundred percent until I knew him better. I also knew I could head back to the café and find a willing audience there who'd listen to my story. But I ached to tell Gideon. Maybe because he seemed somewhat savvy about investigations. I don't know. But I wanted to talk to him.

I pulled out my phone and tapped his number. He answered on the first ring, surprising me. The sound of his voice, deep and alluring, sent butterflies into my stomach. Never in my wildest dreams did I think I'd experience something like that at my age. "Hello Gideon. It's Daisy."

"Yes, my lovely. I'm aware of that."

I wondered if demons had ESP or something. Though he'd denied it, I still wasn't quite sure if he could read my mind. Maybe he knew that I was going to call before I even did. "How did you know it was me?"

He chuckled. "Caller ID?"

Yes, I'm smart enough that I should have realized that. But in my defense, this was my first time calling a demon, and my head was already full with the things I wanted to tell him. "Right," I said. "I was just kidding."

I rolled my eyes at my idiocy, which he could probably see right through.

"What's up, lovely Daisy? Did you visit with Oriana?"

"No. She wasn't home. But I saw Katelyn. I don't know if I told you, but she was also in line to become Fern's replacement."

"Yes, I remember you speaking about her."

His voice really did sound lovely. "She let me know that Carl and Merry weren't as well off as Merry wanted everyone to believe. That Merry didn't control her spending any more than she did her drinking."

The line went silent for a few moments. "That changes things, doesn't it? It seems as though Carl's motivation for killing his wife just got stronger."

I grinned, proud of my new sleuthing skills. "Oh, that's nothing. I headed straight to Carl and Merry's house after that, since it was just up the hill. Carl *was* home, and I convinced him to let me in."

Though I was a little embarrassed about the underhanded way that I'd used to gain entrance, so I kept that part to myself.

"Good girl," Gideon said, and I detected a note of pride in his voice. "Though just for future reference, you may want to be careful and not enter a possible murderer's home without protection. I would be more than happy to accompany you while I'm in town."

I didn't need the reminder that his presence was time-limited. "Thank you, but I was fine. I did have my magically altered pepper spray with me, which would allow me ample time to escape if I needed to."

He cleared his throat. "Still, please consider calling me next time."

My cheeks warmed. "Okay."

A second passed before he spoke again. "I'm eagerly awaiting to hear what you've learned."

Time once more to be bold and brave. "Actually, could we meet somewhere? I'd really like to tell you in person."

I held my breath, waiting for his answer. Yes, I knew he was sort of interested in me, though I wasn't exactly sure why, but from what I'd learned about the male species, guys liked to do the pursuing.

Not that I *was* pursuing. That would be pointless since he was leaving before long anyway.

"I'm at your disposal. Name the time and place."

He seemed pleased with my suggestion, and I smiled. I glanced at my watch. I still had some time before the afternoon rush would kick in. Though it truly wasn't much of a rush this early in May. "I have time now, if you do."

"Absolutely. Do you have a place in mind? If not, my hotel is always available."

The memory of me telling Corey that I wouldn't go anywhere alone with Gideon flared red in my mind. "Uh..."

"There's a lovely patio out back. Sunny. Beautiful flowers. It's quiet this time of day, so we won't be bothered."

I relaxed my shoulders. "Sounds perfect. I can be there in about five minutes."

"I'll be waiting for you."

We ended the call, and I shook my head. This wasn't a romantic meeting. Definitely not a date. We were...working a case together.

I really liked the sound of that. Intrigue. And mystery. All in the desperate attempt to clear my name and bring the killer to justice.

Several minutes later, I strolled through the hotel lobby and out a door that led to the back patio.

Gideon sat in a brown wicker chair with his face to the sun and his eyes closed. He must have sensed me because the moment I stepped from inside, he opened them and looked at me. The smile that followed tugged hard on the ol' heart.

He stood and strode toward me, meeting me halfway. He held out his hands in greeting, and I took them. Before I realized it, he'd pulled me into a hug and kissed the side of my head near my temple.

Then he released me and met my gaze. "Your hair smells divine."

I was sure my cheeks were bright red. "Oh...well. Thank you."

He dipped his head in acknowledgement and gestured with his hand toward where he'd been sitting. "Can I have the hotel staff bring something? A coffee, perhaps?"

I shook my head, and he smiled. "It's not as good as yours, anyway."

I sat in the seat diagonal from his, but it wasn't until he'd sat as well that I realized our knees were close enough to bump.

He captured my gaze. "I'm very eager to hear."

I nodded. "To pick up from where I left off, I have to say Carl said several things that make me very suspicious of him. Things I'm certain he didn't tell the police."

He pointed a finger at me. "See? People will tell non-police personnel much more sometimes. Especially if they have something to conceal."

I wasn't sure what to do with my hands so I folded them in my lap. "I think he does have something to hide. At first, I didn't know if he'd let me in, so I may have suggested—"

He leaned forward. "Suggested what?"

It seemed that I was about to divulge my embarrassing tactics after all. "I asked him if Merry's ghost was in the house. He acted like that would be the worst thing ever. I think his words were, 'God, I hope not', or something like that, which doesn't exactly portray a grieving husband."

He smiled and shook his head. "No, it does not."

"I told him that I could investigate and smudge for him, if he wanted. Which he did. I also crafted a headache potion because he was hung over, so I did help him even if I lied to get into the house. While in the throes of pain, he told me that she was basically an awful person, that he should miss her, but he made it pretty clear that he was relieved she was gone."

Gideon leaned back against the brown wicker chair and studied me. "Fine work, Detective Daisy. Good to think on your feet like that. I believe it will serve you well."

I chuckled then and shook my head. Was this really my life right now?

He narrowed his gaze and gave me an inquisitive smile. "Was there humor that I missed?"

"No. I was just musing about my life and the fact that I'm not at the café but sitting on a sunny patio with a demon discussing a murder. Honestly, I'm not entirely sure that I'm not dreaming."

He reached over and took my hand. "If anyone is dreaming, it's me."

How did I even respond to that?

I chose to skip right past his comment. "Merry had fragments of bone in her witch supplies. I don't know if you're aware, but those are only used for dark magic."

He nodded sagely. "Yes. She would have required those to complete the ritual that sealed our contract."

His words caught me by surprise once again. "Oh. I didn't know that."

"How would you? You're not the type to reach out for a deal with the devil."

I nodded. "That's very true."

We stared at each other for several long moments. If I'd been with anyone else, I would have made my excuses and headed out. But I found that I didn't want to leave Gideon, that I truly enjoyed our time together.

He listened to me with his full attention. Like what I said was important. And he made me feel pretty. All heady stuff that I wasn't used to.

He clapped his hands together. "What are you doing for the rest of the day?"

I thought of the café and that I'd promised Aeri and Nicole that I'd be back. "I probably should go back to work."

"Aeri and Nicole can't handle things?"

I shrugged. "I'm sure they could, but..."

He searched my eyes. "When was the last time you took a day off, Daisy?"

I rubbed my temple as I thought. "I don't know. It's been a while. Probably right after my mom's surgery."

"But taking care of someone is not a break, is it?"

No, it definitely hadn't been. "It's, you know, hard to leave a new business. No one is going to run the cafe better than I can."

He lifted his chin and gazed down at me. "How long has Meowkins been in business? And don't lie to me because I will know."

I widened my eyes. "You *can* read my thoughts, can't you?"

He chuckled, seeming amused by my question. "No, but Nicole mentioned that Meowkins is in its seventh year of operation. Hardly what I'd call a new business."

I opened my mouth to speak and then closed it. I had very little left to argue with. "I told my staff that I'd be back."

He tilted his head. "Look, I'm not going to pressure you into spending time with me. Though it may seem like I am. I merely thought it would be enjoyable to see the sights of Sweet Mountain Meadows with someone who knows the town well. If you must go back to work, I understand."

He really had me backed into a corner because what he'd suggested sounded like the most wonderful day. I hesitated. "I suppose I could call and see if everything is going well."

He grinned. "Fabulous idea."

NINETEEN

Aeri and Nicole had indeed been fine and had encouraged me to take the afternoon off. After a delightful stroll around town, Gideon suggested ice cream to end our day together, which of course, sounded wonderful to me.

I stepped into the ice cream parlor filled with scents of vanilla, caramel and fudge, and my heart felt like it might burst with happiness. I hadn't had such a good day in far too long. Life had become all about work and taking care of the kitties.

Don't get me wrong. Freya and my foster babies brought me a lot of joy. The innocence of a kitten's soft toe beans, or the love shining from the eyes of a grateful older cat kept my heart pure.

But today had been just for me. And it had been wonderful.

Gideon placed his hand on the small of my back and guided me toward the line at the counter. There were only two other people ahead of us, so it wouldn't take long. "What will you have, my lovely Daisy?"

I glanced at the menu overhead. It was hard to decide because all the flavors were so good. Then movement from the corner of my eye caught my attention, and I found Grover hunched over a large sundae, eating it one small bite at a time.

I nudged Gideon with my elbow and leaned close. "That's Grover, Fern's husband. He was the one who watched over our things during the festival."

Gideon glanced at him. "I see. Do you think he might have any information for you?"

I shrugged. "I won't know if I don't ask."

"I'll order for us, and you go talk to him."

I nodded with excitement. "I'll have a scoop of strawberry in a waffle cone."

He winked at me. "Got it."

I strolled over to Grover, trying to act casual, and sat down in the empty seat across from him. It didn't escape me that I'd taken the spot where Fern would have sat in the past. "Hello, Grover."

He looked up at me and smiled. "Hello, Daisy."

I was disappointed to see him looking rough around the edges. His white beard wasn't as tidy as the last time I'd seen him, and he still looked dreadfully tired. "I hate to bother you."

He shook his head. "No bother. My schedule is fairly free these days."

I gave him a sad smile. "As I'm sure you know, Merry was murdered the night of the festival."

He nodded. "Yes. I was on my way back to the town square when I heard the scream. I went to the station yesterday to give a statement, since I was at the festival the whole night. Though I don't know if I was much help. I did see a lot of people pass by, but nothing stood out as suspicious."

Good to know. "I actually wanted to ask you about the ones who stopped in at the booth instead."

He gave me a gravely concerned look. "Because your knife was the murder weapon?" he asked in a low voice.

I glanced around, but there wasn't anyone close enough to hear our conversation. "Yes."

"But I heard your alibi is solid, correct?"

I wasn't sure where he'd gotten his information, but gossip spread faster than a summer wildfire on the mountain. "Yes. I should be fine. But it still bothers me that someone used my knife. I've backtracked that evening and decided I either dropped it while I was walking, though the pockets on my cloak are deep, and it would have been hard for something to fall out. Or someone took it from the booth."

He vehemently shook his head. "I have a hard time believing that. The booth is warded against such things."

My head told me the same thing. "I know, but I'm trying to cover all angles. Do you know who cast the spell over it that night?"

"Jocelyn did."

I dropped my shoulders, feeling defeated. "She does have powerful magic that would be hard to break."

He nodded. "Though, now that you mention it, I do recall Fern telling me that a spell can be undone if a person knows how and has an equal or greater power than the witch who cast it."

I tilted my head to the side, happy for the branch that he'd extended that still gave me hope. "True. It's not easy, but it can be done. The question is, who would want to do it?"

He looked at me matter-of-factly. "Whoever wanted to kill Merry, I'd expect."

I snorted softly. I'd meant that who would want to do it...so that they could harm Merry. But whatever. "Okay then. You were at the booth all night. Did anyone get close enough that they could undo the spell?"

He held up a gnarled pointer finger. "I did leave the booth at one point to use the restroom. Oriana covered for me."

My pulse jumped. "Is that so? How long were you gone for?"

His cheeks colored, and he dropped his gaze. "You have to remember that old bodies aren't always as efficient as younger ones."

I blushed right along with him. "Of course. What time was this?"

He looked up at the ceiling and blinked. "I'd say around eleven. The sun had long since set, and the festivities at the bonfires were in full swing."

I gave him a grateful smile. "Thanks for that information. Anyone else who might have had an opportunity to break the spell, maybe while you were there?"

He sucked his teeth as he thought. "Katelyn sat with me for a while. The booth had gotten really busy about eight, and she helped me take items and put them in the cubbies."

I couldn't imagine Katelyn stealing my knife and committing murder, but I wouldn't completely discount her. "Is that it?"

He nodded. "I think so. I'll try to remember more and let you know if I do."

I stood and placed a hand on his shoulder. "You've been very helpful, Grover. Thank you."

He dipped his head. "It's not much, but it's my pleasure."

When I turned, I found Gideon strolling toward me with a cone in each hand. I gestured toward the front, he switched course, and we met at the door. "Let's walk to the park," I said. "It's just around the corner."

The afternoon sun was lovely, but not hot enough to melt our cones immediately. I dragged my tongue across the cool strawberry ice cream and inwardly sighed. So good.

Then I looked up at Gideon to find him smiling at me. "Stop that," I said jokingly, and I *was* joking because I enjoyed every minute of it.

He chuckled and licked his cone.

I caught a drip of pink ice cream with my tongue before I spoke. "Grover told me he did leave the booth for a bit to use the bathroom. Oriana covered for him. It was around eleven when very few people would be using the enchanted booth.

He lifted an intrigued brow. "Interesting. You'd mentioned the booth was warded, though."

"Yes, but as Grover reminded me, although it's difficult, spells can be broken."

We reached the park, and he guided me to a wrought iron bench that rested beneath a great oak tree. He sat close to me and placed his arm along the back of the bench behind me. He'd invaded my personal space, but I didn't mind.

"In my estimation," he said. "Carl appears to have the strongest motive, but Oriana has the means. Which do you think carries more weight?"

There was no question in my mind. "Means. A person can want to commit a crime, but if they don't have a way to do it, then it means nothing."

He nodded. "I agree."

"I need to find a way to get Oriana to talk to me. I'm almost certain she was at home this morning. But if she won't open her door, what can I do?"

He grinned. "My gut tells me you're a resourceful witch. I bet if you try hard, you can think of something."

I narrowed my eyes and frowned at him in jest. "You're a powerful demon. Can't you locate her?"

He chuckled. "Do you want me to use my powers?"

A shiver raced through me, and I realized I had no idea what that would entail. "Maybe? Will it cost me my soul?"

He laughed out loud. "No. I will never ask you to give up your soul."

That settled my nerves. Somewhat.

He reached for the door to my shop but didn't open it. "If you can get me something of Oriana's, a personal item or photo of the two of you together, I'll be able to locate her for you."

I met his gaze. His suggestion seemed far too easy. "Just like that?"

He shrugged. "It will require a bit of effort on my part, but nothing too taxing."

I blinked, wondering if there was something he wasn't saying. "I know there's a photo in my yearbook from school that we're both in. Will that work?"

"It should. Take a picture with your phone's camera and send it to me. I'll let you know if there's a problem."

I couldn't help but smile. "That sounds great."

He pulled open the door. "Good. I'll call you later."

Just as I took my first step inside, he grabbed my hand. I turned back to him to find him watching me intently. He flicked his gaze back and forth between my eyes. "Thank you for a lovely day, Daisy."

Then he leaned forward and kissed me on the cheek, close to the corner of my mouth. His actions stunned me and apparently froze my vocal cords, because I didn't say a word as he turned and strode away.

TWENTY

I'd just started to think that Gideon's attempt to locate Oriana hadn't worked when I caught sight of a woman in the distance who looked very much like her. In fact, she was right where Gideon said she would be, sitting on a bench inside the park with her little dog lying at her feet.

I took the long way to reach Oriana, weaving in and out of trees, so that she wouldn't see me coming and try to run. I'd chase her down if I had to.

When I was close enough that she wouldn't easily get away, I made my way back to the main path. When she came into view again, I realized she wouldn't have seen me coming anyway because she had her head down and several wadded tissues clenched in her hands.

Her little black and white terrier stood as I approached and wagged its tail.

"Oriana?" I said in a quiet voice.

She jerked her gaze up, revealing wet eyelashes and tear-stained cheeks. Her normally windblown hair was a complete disaster, looking as if she hadn't brushed it that morning. Her grief was raw, and I couldn't help but feel sorry for her.

"What do you want?" she asked in a voice that let me know she wasn't happy to see me.

I held up a hand, signaling that I came in peace. "You seemed very distraught, and I wanted to make sure that you're okay."

She blinked her eyes several times and sniffed. "Other than the death of my sister, I'm perfectly fine."

Which obviously, she wasn't. Even though I was certain I wasn't welcome, I walked to the bench and sat, leaving a reasonable amount of distance between us. "I'm very sorry for your loss, Oriana."

She snorted. "No, you're not. You hated her, and it was your knife that killed her."

I shook my head slowly but firmly. "No. The person who *used* my knife killed her. I had nothing to do with that."

By the look in her eyes, I could tell she didn't believe me. "You *hated* her."

I leaned away from her in defense. "Umm...your relationship wasn't that great with her, either, and you were the one found holding my knife, so..."

She burst into tears and buried her face in her hands, leaving me feeling like a heartless person. "I'm sorry. I didn't mean to make you more upset."

She didn't respond, so I tried again. "As much as you dislike me, I think we have one thing in common."

Her cries turned to quieter sobs. "What?" she said, her voice shaky with emotion.

"You say that you didn't kill her, and I say I didn't either. If we're both telling the truth, then someone else is still out there. Someone who left a nasty cloud of suspicion hanging over us."

I said this to appease her, but she was still suspect number one in my book. "I don't think anyone wants that person to go unpunished."

She remained quiet for several moments and then she lifted her head and met my gaze. "No. That person needs to pay."

I sensed the hard shell around her cracking, and it gave me hope. "I know there's a lot of speculation in town about who might have killed her, but you knew her better than most. Who do you think did it?"

She shrugged helplessly. "I have no idea."

I studied her carefully, looking for signs of deceit. "What about Carl? Did she finally push him too far?"

Oriana waved her hands in front of her, dismissing my question. "No. No way."

Except he'd proven to me that he wasn't as devoted as he'd made it seem. "Are you sure?"

"I'm positive. Yes, they had their share of problems. Every couple does. But he was dedicated to her. Gave her everything. You know that."

When I lifted a questioning brow, she continued. "I've known Carl for many years. My sister might have tried his patience, but he's a good man. I know that for certain."

I could see that Oriana truly did believe in his innocence, so I let that question go for now. Carl might have her convinced that he'd never commit murder, but I wasn't so sure.

Instead, I tried a different line of questioning. "I saw Grover yesterday at the ice cream shop. He seems to be doing a little better."

"That's good."

I made sure she was looking at me before I asked my next question so that I could check her reaction. "He told me that you watched the enchanted booth for him while he took a break."

She nodded. "I did."

At least that was confirmed. "I left my cloak there for several hours with my athame in the pocket. While you were watching the booth, did you see anything suspicious? Anyone who might have tried to steal it or break Jocelyn's spell?"

She held my gaze and didn't flinch. But it almost seemed like she was doing it on purpose. "I didn't see anything."

"Did anyone go into the booth while you were there?"

"Katelyn, I guess. Uh, Lilibeth was there, but I don't think she came behind the table."

"But you're not sure?"

She shrugged. "I chatted with several groups of people while I was there. I didn't know I'd be required to report every single thing that I saw, so I wasn't paying particular attention. The booth is warded, so I wasn't worried about anyone taking anything."

I raised my brows. "But someone did steal something." I was ninety-percent sure of that.

"It seems so," she said quietly.

"Oriana, please don't take this the wrong way, but I have to ask. How did you know where to find Merry in a dark forest with not even a full moon overhead? What prompted you to look for her? What led you there?"

She opened her hands, palms up. "I don't know. I left right after you were chosen, and I walked for a bit. I knew Merry would be angry that she hadn't been the one, and I was thinking of a way to tell her. Then I just...found her. I don't know if it was intuition or a sisterly connection that led me to her. But there she was."

Oriana inhaled a sharp breath and dropped her gaze to the ground. She ruffled the fur on her little terrier and seemed to take comfort when the dog licked her hand. "I can't believe she's gone," she whispered.

"Me, either," I said, and I meant it.

Several moments of silence passed before Oriana straightened and looked at me. "I'm sorry that I accused you of stealing my ring, Daisy. When Corey told me about finding it, he'd said he'd notify you, too."

I nodded. "He did. Any idea why Merry would have taken it?"

"None," she said quietly. "It breaks my heart that one of the last things she did was steal from me. That's hard to accept."

I didn't have siblings, but I was certain that would be a huge betrayal.

She dabbed at her eyes, sniffed, and stood. "I need to go. I've been away from the house longer than I'd said I would, and Bill is probably wondering where I am."

I stood as well. "Yeah, I should get back to the café, too. I was just out on a quick break."

I bid her farewell and watched her walk away, studying her as she went. By the pace of her steps, she seemed to be in a hurry to get away from me. Or perhaps Bill was the type of person she didn't want to keep waiting.

My first impression was that her emotions had been genuine and that she hadn't taken her sister's life. But she was still the one with a possible motive and definite means, not to mention opportunity.

I called Gideon on my way back to the parking lot where I'd left my car and was disappointed when he didn't pick up. I tried not to wonder what he was doing and where he was, but I couldn't help it.

Then a text came in a few moments later, and he apologized, saying that he was in the middle of a phone meeting with his boss and that he'd call me later.

A phone meeting with his boss? Hopefully, that didn't mean the head honcho.

I sat in my car for several minutes, pondering what to do. What popped into my mind was something I wouldn't have thought I'd consider, but then again, my life was currently full of things I'd never expected.

I decided to pay a visit to Corey at the police station. He was over the official investigation, after all, and there were a few things that I bet he didn't know.

It didn't take me long to reach the brown brick building not far from the center of town. Stately blue spruce pines and a beautiful green lawn surrounded it, but other than that, landscaping was minimal.

I spoke to the receptionist inside. After she'd confirmed with Sergeant Shelton that it was okay for me to enter, she led me down a hallway and then stopped next to an open door with Corey's name and title on a small sign outside his office. I nodded my thanks and peered inside.

Corey looked up from the open file he'd been focused on and gave me a wide smile. He stood and gestured to a chair in front of his desk. "Please. Have a seat."

We both sat, and I met his gaze. "Thanks for seeing me."

He eyed me closely. "Of course. I've been wondering if you'd call, but an in-person visit is even better."

A blanket of awkwardness snugged in around me. "Well, you said to call if I had anything further to add, and I didn't have until now."

He straightened in his seat, and his warm expression turned serious. "Great. Let's hear it."

I didn't want to tell him everything that I'd learned because most of it was still speculation, and I didn't want him to know that I'd been snooping overly much. But he did need to know some things if I wanted to fully protect myself. "I've recently learned that Oriana and Katelyn Hyde were also in the enchanted booth that night and might have had access to my belongings."

He drummed his fingers on the desk. "Interesting. Neither of them mentioned in their statements that they'd been there."

I shrugged, letting him know that I thought that seemed suspicious. "I wondered if they had or not. I guess Grover didn't let you know, either, when he came in to give his statement. Though, I suppose at that point, he wouldn't have known someone had taken my knife and used it."

"Agreed," he said. "But to be clear, someone would have to break the anti-theft spell if they wanted to take anything that wasn't theirs, correct?"

Again, I was grateful that I didn't have to explain such things to someone outside the witch community. "That's true. But while it might be difficult, it's not impossible to break such a spell."

He slid a notepad toward him. "Good to know," he said as he scrawled notes. Then he glanced up at me. "We'll follow up with all of them."

"Great. Thank you. I appreciate everything you're doing to help clear my name."

"It sounds like you're looking into things a little yourself."

Guilty. "Yeah. A little. I figure people might not be so nervous to have a conversation with me, and they might remember more."

It was close to what Gideon had told me.

He dropped his pen and placed his forearms on the desk, leaning closer to me. "That's possible."

His intuitive stare began to make me feel nervous again, and I gathered my purse. "I should go."

"You know, Daisy, you and I should go for a drink or dinner sometime. I'd like to catch up with you."

I swallowed a big ball of nerves. "Uh, sure. Maybe after you finish your investigation? It's probably not a good idea to go now since I'm on the suspect list."

He smiled and nodded. "I look forward to it."

I made my way to the door and glanced back. "I'll see you later."

He leaned back in his chair with a satisfied look on his face. "Yes, you will."

I cursed my luck as I quickly exited the police station. Why? Why, why, why? Why couldn't he have been interested years ago? Now, he did nothing but complicate my life.

But only if I let him, I countered, reminding myself that I was in charge of my destiny. But how did I not let him affect me when there was a tiny part of me that still liked him? Up until a few days ago, I'd accepted that a romantic relationship would never be in my future.

But now that hope I'd had as a young woman had been rekindled. I did like Gideon, but he would leave me soon, not to mention the fact that he was a demon.

Corey made me nervous, but part of that could be because of the investigation. Obviously, I didn't know him well at all, either. But maybe once Gideon was gone, I might find that I wanted to.

One thing was for sure. I needed to get back to Meowkins. I'd neglected my café more than I ever had, and I was starting to feel antsy about it.

TWENTY-ONE

When I walked into Meowkins a little after noon, the coffee shop was nearly empty, but the Purry Parlor was full. Not surprising, since it was a Saturday afternoon. Through the glass doors, I spotted moms and dads with kids and some very playful kitties.

I waved to Aeri behind the counter and headed for the backroom to stow my things and wash my hands.

The cats loved Saturdays when they got a lot of attention. Except, Old Grey. He was too tired to interact much, and he'd often climb up the shelves I'd hung on the wall that gave the cats a place to perch and watch.

To be honest, he'd probably rubbed against Nicole's legs, asking her to put him up there because jumping was no longer easy for him.

It occurred to me then that perhaps I should adopt Old Grey myself so that he would know the joys of a forever home before he crossed the rainbow bridge. He could still come to the café every day with me and Freya so that he wouldn't be alone, even though he slept most of the day and didn't require much company.

I tied a brown and pink apron around me and headed out to the front. Aeri finished with a customer and turned her attention to me. "Everything okay? You sure hurried out of here in a rush."

It was true that I had left without saying much. "Sorry. I guess I should just tell you. Gideon has been helping me with my investigations, and I've had trouble pinning down Oriana, as you know."

She nodded, her straight dark brown hair brushing her shoulders as she did. "Right. So, Gideon called?"

"Not exactly. Well, yes, he did, but he was letting me know that this...spell that he helped me with had worked. It was one that would allow us to track Oriana if she left her house."

Aeri lifted her brows in interest. "I've never heard of that one."

I tilted my head from side to side, hoping I wouldn't regret my next words. "It's something new, and it requires a witch...and a demon to complete it."

"A witch and a *demon*?" She leaned close to me. "I never would have guessed he's a demon. I guess because I've never met one before. That's kind of cool. And scary. Are you safe around him?"

Now, I understood why Gideon hadn't told many people. "Yes, he's perfectly fine. He's a regular person with a...unique job."

She nodded. "Why didn't you tell me sooner?"

I shrugged, feeling guilty. There were few things that I'd kept from my best friend. "He barely confessed it to me, and I guess I was worried that you might have a negative reaction to him."

She released a sigh. "I guess I did, sort of. I really don't know that much about his type, and most of the stories that I've heard make them sound like monsters."

"Same. But now I wonder if the people telling the stories had brokered a deal with a demon and later regretted it. Perhaps they had personal vendettas."

Aeri leaned against the counter and seemed to consider my point. "Makes sense, doesn't it? I guess other demons might not be as pleasant as Gideon. He's quite nice."

I thought of our walk around town the previous day and smiled. "I completely agree."

She chuckled. "I think Brad was right. You've met your match with this one."

My happiness faded, and I shook my head. "No, I'm afraid not. He'll be leaving town soon."

Aeri's smile faded. "Really? That's too bad. Can't he come back?"

I shrugged. "I don't know. Besides, long distance relationships never last. He told me he likes me, but that doesn't mean much, does it? Not when he lives in Oregon."

Aeri raised hopeful brows. "Oregon isn't *that* far away. And who knows, maybe if he likes it here, he'd consider moving."

I chuckled then and shook my head. "I think we're getting way ahead of ourselves. Thinking he might move here is a little far-fetched. Just because he's the most decent guy I've met in a long time does not mean we're destined to be together. Let's not resort to desperation."

Sadness dimmed her usually bright eyes. "I just want you to be happy, Daisy. You deserve that."

I snorted. "I am happy, Aeri. I love my life."

She lifted a shoulder and let it drop. "I know, but..."

I flipped my expression into a happy smile. "Plus, I've accepted this new coven responsibility. I have a feeling my life is going to be very full from here on out."

As much as I hadn't wanted to be chosen to serve, the idea of it had begun to settle. So far, no one in the coven had asked anything of me, but I expected that would change once I attended an official council meeting.

Aeri did smile then. "That is pretty cool, and yes, you'll likely be busy."

The bell above the door chimed, and we both glanced toward it. My favorite customer walked through the door. "Afternoon, Gilbert. Are you here for your free coffee?"

He grinned and shrugged. "Might as well take advantage of it while I can."

I matched his grin. "Absolutely. An Americano?"

He glanced at the board overhead. "I was thinking of something with a little less caffeine since it's later in the day. How about a caramel macchiato?"

Through the window behind him, I spotted Katelyn strolling past the café, and my pulse jumped. I really wanted to talk to her again, to confront her about being in the booth that night and possibly having access to my knife.

I glanced back at Gilbert. "We'll get right on that."

When he sauntered away, Aeri leaned close. "That's the third time he's been in today."

I chuckled. "It's alright. Hey, I just saw Katelyn walk by. I need to talk to her."

Aeri nodded encouragingly. "Yeah. Go."

Gilbert looked up as I strode to the door. "Aeri will have that for you shortly."

Then I headed outside into the bright sunshine and glanced in the direction Katelyn had walked. I spotted the back of her head and hurried after her. She'd already put a fair amount of distance between us, and I remembered that she liked to power walk.

I stepped up my pace and then began to jog. If I didn't, she'd disappear before I could catch her.

But my plan worked, and I called out to her just as she was about to cross the street and head to the next block. She looked back, and I waved so that she'd know I was the one who'd called out.

She smiled and waved back.

By the time I reached her, I was more than a little out of breath. "Hi," I managed and then paused to fill my lungs.

She gave me a knowing look. "You need to start walking more, or you're going to be old before you know it."

I knew she was right, but I cast off her comment with a shake of my head.

She chuckled. "This must be important if you're willing to race down the street after me."

I released another breath and could feel my pulse slowing. "It is. I wanted to ask you..." I inhaled again. "Grover said that you'd been in the enchanted booth with him for a while at the festival."

She frowned. "Yes, I was. It was busy, and he needed help."

I licked my dry lips. "Right. But that's where I'd stored my knife, too. I didn't have it again after that."

She studied me for a long moment. Then she straightened, and her expression filled with incredulity. "Are you asking me if I took it? If I murdered Merry?"

I sort of was, but I denied it. "No. I just want to know if you saw anyone suspicious hanging around."

"No one out of the ordinary. Sure, there were people at the festival that I didn't know, but none hung around looking like they were up to something."

My side ached, and I pushed my thumb into it. "Were you there when Oriana took over for Grover?"

She shook her head. "No, though I did see her walk by with Merry and their husbands."

As had I. I bit my bottom lip, trying to think of what to ask next. "Carl never came near the booth that you saw?"

Again, she shook her head. "Daisy, why aren't you letting the police handle this? That's their job."

I replied with a sharp look. "Don't tell me if your reputation and possibly your life was on the line that you wouldn't do whatever you could to clear your name."

Her features softened. "Fair enough."

I hated to gossip about others, but I was getting nowhere. "The reason I asked about Carl is because I stopped off at his house after talking to you. We both know that he and Merry had their issues, but Katelyn, he pretty much told me that he's glad that she's gone."

She drew her brows together in surprise. "He did?"

"Yeah. He made living with her sound like a nightmare. I really have to wonder if he might have killed his wife."

She blinked several times as she processed the information. "I just can't picture that. He's always been the nicest person and so patient with her antics."

I could tell that my statement had gotten to her, so I continued to push. "I wonder if he'd finally snapped. People can be pushed past their limits, you know."

She nodded then and met my gaze. "This probably won't surprise you to learn, but Merry cheated on Carl. Several times. Probably more."

I exhaled in disbelief. "Why didn't you mention that before?"

Her cheeks pinkened. "I guess I was trying to protect Carl. I really don't think he could do something so sinister, and I knew if I'd brought it up, he'd become their prime suspect."

Like he'd become mine. "But what if you're really covering for a murderer without realizing it?"

She widened her eyes as the color drained from her face.

And she accused *me* of taking things into my own hands? "You need to tell the police about what you know."

She nodded, and I could tell her thoughts were running wild, so I pressed on. "I would go right now, if I was you. You don't want them to think you aided or abetted him."

Katelyn gasped. "No. No, I'll go as soon as I drop off this letter at the post office."

Without saying anything further, she hustled off, power walking like a boss.

My pulse had picked up again during our discussion, and my heartbeats thudded in my ears. I was onto something here. I could feel it in my bones.

I wanted to drive straight to Carl's house, but I'd told Gideon I'd wait for him. Still, how was I supposed to do that if he didn't call me back?

TWENTY-TWO

I couldn't tell if Gideon had sensed my need or what, but he'd suddenly called and then drove to my place to pick me up. When we reached Carl's house, Gideon pulled into the drive and parked much like I had before. Everything looked the same with one exception. I pointed toward Merry's black SUV that sat off to the side of the driveway. "Looks like Carl might be planning to sell Merry's car."

He glanced over at it. "Why do you think that?"

I shrugged. "Last time I was here, it was in the garage."

We exited Gideon's lovely Mercedes and headed for the sidewalk ahead, but before we turned onto it, he paused. I stumbled to a stop and turned to look back at him. He'd tilted his head as he stared at the garage that was open a foot from the ground. Then he squatted and looked inside.

He swiveled his head and met my gaze with an intrigued one of his own. "Perhaps he moved it to make room for a new car, because there are two vehicles parked inside this garage."

I scrunched my features in surprise. "That doesn't make any sense. Why would he need three cars? I mean, let's just say he did decide to buy a new one, why wouldn't he trade in Merry's? One person does not need three vehicles."

He stood and shrugged. "Let's ask him."

I thought for a second and then strode toward the garage. "I wonder what the new kind is?"

I'd started to bend down when Gideon caught my arm. "Permit me."

He dropped to his hands and knees, but ended up lying chest down on the ground so that he could see better. I felt bad that he had to lay on the dusty cement to see inside. It would mess up his nice gray shirt, but he didn't seem to mind. "There's a white truck and a dark blue sedan. Judging by the amount of dirt on their rims, I'd say that neither of them are new. That or the business where Carl purchased it from doesn't clean their vehicles before selling them."

While I considered this new information, he got to his feet, dusted off his shirt and pants, and then his hands. I shuffled through my memories of everyone I knew who drove that kind of a car, but I could only come up with one person. "Gideon. Oriana drives a dark blue sedan."

He lifted an intrigued brow. "Is that so? Perhaps she's visiting?"

I rejected his notion with a narrowed gaze. "There's no reason to put her car in the garage, especially if he had to move Merry's to do it. There's a reason they're hiding it."

"Good point," he conceded. "I say we knock on the door and see if she is indeed in the house."

I linked my arm through his and tugged him in that direction. "Let's do it."

We rang the bell and knocked several times, but no one answered. "He's not going to open the door," I said.

Gideon tossed aside my complaint with a small shake of his head, and he rang the bell again several times in a row. "Patience, my lovely. And persistence. If we stay and continue knocking, he'll begin to understand that we aren't going away. Then he'll open the door but will try to get us to leave as quickly as possible."

As soon as Gideon finished speaking, I heard the distinct sound of a lock being turned, and Carl opened the door. I shot Gideon an amazed look, and he responded with an almost imperceptible lift of a corner of his mouth.

Carl glanced back and forth between us. "What's the emergency?"

Gideon looked at me as if to remind me it was my investigation.

I pinned Carl with a hard look. "The emergency is that your wife is dead, and you weren't completely honest with me."

He snorted and shook his head. "I don't have time for this. Let the police do their job."

Carl tried to shut the door, but Gideon placed the toe of his shoe inside the door frame, preventing Carl from closing it. "Give Daisy the courtesy of listening to her."

Carl inhaled a deep breath, puffing out his chest, ready for a verbal battle, but when he met Gideon's gaze, he immediately backed down.

At that moment, I couldn't have been more grateful to have Gideon on my side. "That's right. You can let us in and hear me out, or I'll go straight to the police with the information I've received. What's it going to be?"

I could not believe those words had come out of my mouth, but they had. I supposed Gideon's presence had given me the bravado to speak them.

Carl narrowed his eyes at me, letting me know I was pushing my limits, but he didn't look at Gideon again. "I'll give you five minutes, and then you need to leave me alone."

With a huff, he stood back and opened the door. We stepped inside the entryway, and it became clear that he had no intentions of inviting us farther inside the house.

Whatever. I could work with this. "I've learned recently, Carl, that Merry was guilty of cheating on you."

He didn't seem shocked, which annoyed me.

"Many, many times," I added to check his reaction, and this time, he flinched. Honestly, I had no idea how many lovers she'd had, but

I needed to shake up Carl if I wanted to get past the wall that he'd built between us.

Anger reddened his cheeks. "What is this, Daisy? An opportunity to smear my dear wife's name more than you already have? I didn't want to think you'd held the knife that killed her, but I'm starting to wonder."

It was a bluff to get us to leave, and I knew it. He wasn't going to intimidate me with his meaningless threats. I leaned closer to him. "Don't tell me that you were unaware of her affairs, because I already know that's not the case. That, along with the things you said about Merry the day after her death, makes you look very suspicious."

He shook his head to deny my accusations, but then he must have reconsidered. "This is all pointless. You know I didn't kill her."

Gideon cleared his throat. "That doesn't seem to be the case."

Carl still wouldn't acknowledge him and kept his gaze locked on me. "Look, Merry might have made my life miserable, but I didn't kill her. I'll admit I thought about leaving her, but that doesn't make me a murderer."

I lifted an inquisitive brow. "Yes, but we both know that Merry spent all your money. If you divorced, she'd get as much alimony as she could, and you'd still be giving her a lot."

He shook his head, unwilling to concede. "I didn't kill her."

I was running out of scare tactics and glanced up at Gideon. He gave me a small nod and focused on Carl. "Perhaps you can tell us why Oriana's car is in your garage, then."

Carl choked and sputtered until Gideon clapped him on the back. "Take your time," Gideon said. "We're in no hurry."

After a moment, Carl had composed himself well enough to speak. "Her car is here because I'd told her I'd change the brakes on it."

I looked at him with incredulity. He really was tightening that noose around his throat. "That's funny because Oriana's husband has a fleet of construction vehicles that he maintains. Why wouldn't she ask him?"

Carl stammered, and I heard movement from deeper in the house. He turned and shook his head, but that didn't prevent Oriana from showing herself. "You're right," she said to me. "That's not the reason I'm here."

Carl continued to shake his head, but Oriana approached and took Carl's hand.

I gaped in astonishment. That one small act was a huge revelation.

Poor Oriana still looked as messed up as she had earlier, but I wondered how much of her angst came from the fact that she had a relationship with Carl and was in danger of being a prime suspect, instead of from her sister's death.

Gideon snorted. "Please do explain yourself."

Oriana turned to Carl. "It's time to tell the truth. You know as well as I do that this will come out. Especially now."

Then she looked at me. "It's true. Carl and I have been seeing each other for a while now."

Unbelievable. "How long is a while?"

Oriana turned to Carl, and he looked at me. "Years. And yes, I know what it looks like, but neither of us killed Merry. We've both been content to keep our marriages intact while continuing to see each other."

Oriana blushed. "You see, one of the affairs that Merry had was with *my* husband. Carl and I had been talking one day, and, in the heat of the moment, we'd decided that fair play was fair play. But afterward, we realized we really did like each other."

Carl turned to me, and I caught hints of anger sparking in his eyes. "At first, it felt good to sneak behind her back. She deserved it. Then I realized that Oriana is everything that Merry wasn't."

Gideon narrowed his eyes in suspicion. "Why did you not both divorce then and be together? Wouldn't a happy life with each other be the ultimate revenge?"

That was the exact question I'd been about to ask.

Oriana sighed. "Like Carl said, we'd thought about it, and maybe we still would have at some point. But Merry would take a lot of Carl's money, while I'd be shackled with half of Bill's debt."

I shook my head. "You do realize that makes you both look very guilty."

Oriana sighed. "I know, but we're not. We have an alibi during the time Merry was killed."

"And what would that be?" I prompted.

Carl glanced at Oriana, and she nodded for him to proceed. "We were in the woods together," he said. "After that disaster with Merry making a complete fool of herself, I didn't go home like I'd said. I texted Oriana, and she met me not far from your circle. We stayed together until it was time for her to head there."

I cast them a dubious look. "That's not exactly a good alibi since you both had strong reasons to want her out of your lives. What if you were in on it together?"

Oriana held up a hand. "Someone else can confirm this. Actually, two people."

Carl nodded. "Lilibeth and her boyfriend caught us together, and we all made a deal to not speak of it. She was worried her mom would find out and freak out because she'd forbidden her to see her boyfriend. And of course, it would only create more problems if our affair came to light. Our reputations. Oriana's marriage. Trust me, dealing with Merry's death has been enough of an ordeal."

Even if what they were saying was true, it didn't quite pan out. "If Merry's death was such an ordeal to you both, then why aren't you interested in helping the police find out who killed her?"

Oriana looked as if my words were bullets that mortally wounded her. "Of course, we want to find her killer. Despite everything, she didn't deserve to die."

Some might argue that. "Did Merry ever find out about the two of you?"

A look of guilt landed on her face, and she shifted a sideways glance at Carl.

He rubbed his eyes, stretching out the bags beneath them. "We don't know. She never confronted either of us."

Oriana released an almost imperceptible sigh. "But I think I might have lost my ring here in the house. I didn't consider that when I found it missing, but now that it was discovered in Merry's purse, I wonder. Perhaps she did know about our affair."

Gideon nodded. "I agree that it's probable. She was likely trifling with you when she blamed Daisy, knowing that it would raise your anger against her."

Oriana nodded. "Makes sense. That's why she didn't care to stay at the coffee shop that morning after she'd finished embarrassing Daisy. Staying wouldn't have solved anything with the ring because Merry had it all along."

I folded my arms and looked at Gideon, wondering what his opinion was of everything. Personally, I was mildly convinced that they told the truth. Though if neither of them was guilty, I had no clue who was.

Gideon met my gaze. "I think we've learned all that we need here. We should go."

I nodded.

Carl held up a hand. "Could I ask a favor? I would like to be the one to go to the police with this. It will only look more suspicious if they find out from other sources."

I studied him for a long moment, trying to decide if that was a wise move, and then nodded. "I'll give you until tomorrow."

Oriana's eyes watered, and she blinked rapidly. "Thank you."

With that, Gideon took my hand and led me from the house. Outside, I glanced up at him. "That was interesting."

His fingers tightened around mine. "Very. How do you feel about a drive up the canyon? I'd like to see it while I have the chance, and we can review facts and see where that leads us."

I glanced at our hands clasped together, to where his long fingers wrapped around mine, to where mine curled around his as well. I wasn't sure what was between us, but I liked it. "Let's do it."

TWENTY-THREE

Bright sunshine warmed the interior of the Mercedes, and Gideon lowered the windows to compensate. Fresh mountain air blew in, bringing with it the scents of pine and earth. I filled my lungs and leaned back against the luxurious leather seats. "I need a car like this."

Gideon chuckled. "You may drive mine whenever you like."

Except that he'd be leaving soon, and I didn't want to think about that. "How did the call go with your boss?"

He shrugged. "It was okay. He'd spoken to his boss, the Prince of Darkness, about the things that have happened here. They're concerned."

I shifted a sideways glance at him, relieved that there was a middle man between him and the devil. "Because someone was able to kill Merry when they shouldn't have been?"

"Yes, we discussed that and a few other things."

I put thoughts of Gideon's departure to the side and focused on the murder. "I hate to say it because it leaves us nowhere, but I think Carl and Oriana might be telling the truth."

He looked at me and lifted his chin. "I do, as well."

Disappointment rolled through me. I'd thought for sure we'd figured it out. "I don't know where to go from here."

He didn't turn his gaze to me, but a smile curved his lips and gave me hope. "Are you easily dissuaded from things that you want?"

I frowned and considered his question. "I don't think so."

But maybe I was. Maybe I'd taken what life had handed me for the most part and not fought for what I'd wanted.

"Then don't give up now," he said.

Easy for him to say. "But what do we do? We've reached a dead end."

He flicked another glance in my direction. "Have we, though? We've certainly closed off one avenue, but that doesn't mean there aren't others."

I accepted his words and searched my mind for ideas. "Do you mean Katelyn?"

He effortlessly cruised around a tight corner in the road and shrugged. "Could be. Who else carries a hint of suspicion? Who else was around that night and might have a vested interest in having Merry out of the picture?"

I dug deep into my thoughts. "Lilibeth had been hovering around the booth. Had maybe gone inside, though I can't think why she'd kill Merry, and if Carl and Oriana have an alibi, then so does she."

He nodded thoughtfully. "Who else?"

I opened my hands wide in exasperation. "Our high priestess Jocelyn did seem to be very happy that I was chosen. Maybe she wanted Merry out of the picture."

He slowed as we took another corner. "Any reason that you know of why she would be biased against Merry?"

"No," I said slowly as the gears in my head turned. "But Grover said she was the one who'd warded the enchanted booth."

A smile spread across his lips. "See? There's another avenue to investigate already. You just had to put your mind to it."

I shook my head. "I can't picture Jocelyn committing murder. She's been around a long time, and she seems content to let the universe unfold as it chooses. I can't begin to imagine her messing with fate."

He sighed. "Let's keep thinking then."

A stubborn thought circled in my head, growing stronger. "I suppose if I'm investigating, I should still follow up with Jocelyn, right? Just to be sure her view of events matches everyone else's."

He reached over and patted my leg. "I would agree with that."

"Great. As soon as we're near the top where I can get cell service, I'm going to call her."

I tried to relax as we cruised along the winding road through dense lodgepole and pinyon pines along with an abundance of aspens. It was a beautiful day, possibly one of my last with Gideon, and it seemed a shame to waste it all thinking about a grisly murder.

When he reached the end of the road and the ski resort that was now closed for the season, he pulled into the empty parking lot and turned off the engine. "Do you mind if we get out for a moment? I would like to take in the full view."

"Of course not."

He insisted on opening my door for me, so I waited patiently until he reached my side of the car and tugged it open. He held out a hand for me, and I took it, even though I was perfectly capable of climbing out of a car on my own. I met his gaze and smiled. "Thank you."

We stood at the edge of the parking lot, and he rotated a full circle, gazing up at the mountains around us and the blue sky overhead. "You're lucky to live in such a beautiful place. In Oregon, we have many trees as well. That's part of the reason I chose to relocate there."

I glanced around, trying to see my hometown through his eyes. Dark green and dusty blue pines were interspersed with the bright green of the aspen leaves. In the fall, the aspens would turn yellow, and look even more spectacular. At the very tops of the mountain ahead of us, patches of white snow remained and would likely do so into June. Even though the sun was out, the peaks of the mountains were much chillier than our current altitude.

I shifted my gaze to him. "What's the rest of the reason you decided to move to Oregon?"

His smile was warm and genuine. "My nephew resides there. Really, he's more like a son than anything. His parents died when he was young, so I cared for him until he was older."

"Do you have other children?"

He scoffed. "No. I've never been inclined to settle down with any one woman. Caring for Lucas was quite enough for me."

His response gave me great insight into his mind, and it was an arrow to my heart. He wasn't the kind of man who was interested in a serious relationship. Not that I thought that would be our future, but part of me had wondered. And maybe even hoped.

I forced a smile and pointed to a row of pines nearby. "There's a little lake just beyond those trees. Would you like to see it?"

He grinned and held out his hand. "Yes, of course. Lead the way my lovely Daisy."

I took his hand, feeling the bittersweet tug of emotion, and we stepped up onto the sidewalk. From there, we followed a trail of wooden planks until we reached the pond.

He didn't release my hand. Instead, he held it tightly as we gazed across the smooth surface of the water that reflected the trees and mountains. He inhaled a deep breath and released it. "Magnificent."

I watched him, thinking the same thing.

We stayed that way for a while, just taking in the sights and not speaking. Then he glanced down at me. "I suppose reality calls, doesn't it?"

Unfortunately, he'd nailed that right on the head. "I suppose it does. I guess I'll try to reach Jocelyn now before we head into the canyon and I lose service."

He agreed with a nod. I pulled out my phone as we strode back to his car and called Jocelyn.

She answered after a few rings. "Blessed be, Daisy. How are you on this fine afternoon?"

I envied the gift of grace and peace that always emanated from her. "It *is* a very fine afternoon, Jocelyn, thank you. I'm sorry to bother you."

Jocelyn tsked. "Of course, it's not a bother. I've been meaning to call you as well to see when we can get together and talk about your new calling. Though I've felt as if you've been particularly busy these past few days."

I snorted, reminding myself that her intuition was one of the reasons we'd accepted her as our leader. "A little busy. If it's okay, I just have a quick question, and then we can talk later about setting a date."

"Of course. Ask me anything."

"Grover said you cast the protection spell on the enchanted booth for Beltane. Did you encounter any problems? Or any interruptions?"

"Ah. You're concerned how someone managed to take your knife. Yes, well, I must tell you that you have some incorrect information. I was not asked to cast the spell. I imagine Grover must have his witches confused. Understandable, of course."

I glanced at Gideon and widened my eyes. He did the same, and I could tell he was eager for information. "Oh, I see," I said to Jocelyn. "I'm sure you're right, and I will touch base with Grover again."

We said our goodbyes, and I pocketed my phone. Then I turned to Gideon with my pulse pounding in my chest. "Jocelyn never cast the spell. She thinks Grover is confused about who he'd asked."

Gideon lifted his brow. "Confused? Or never had the spell cast in the first place? Perhaps he doesn't want to admit he forgot to ask."

An unwanted conclusion slipped into my thoughts. "Or perhaps he didn't want one to be cast at all."

I hated to consider the idea that the sweet old man might be capable of murder. Worse, that he'd chosen my knife to kill Merry. "I guess we need to talk to him again if we want the truth."

He tipped his head to me. "Indeed, we do."

TWENTY-FOUR

I directed Gideon to Grover's house, and he parked along the curb. As we made our way to the front door, I found that Fern's gardens hadn't been cared for. Weeds had sprouted everywhere, and perennials that usually thrived were shrunken, brown shadows of their former selves.

Gideon stepped onto the dried grass near the front porch and crouched down near another garden. "This is concerning."

I agreed that it was a shame that Fern's plants hadn't been cared for. As dedicated as Grover had seemed to her memory, his actions in this case seemed out of place. "I expect he's likely suffered from some depression. He and Fern had been together a long time."

Gideon stood and met my gaze. "No, that's not what I mean. It's still early in the year. Temperatures here are not hot enough to outright kill these types of plants."

I frowned at him, trying to understand. "I suppose, but..."

He wrapped his fingers around my upper arm and stared into my eyes. "There is something sinister at play, Daisy. Something unnatural."

I shivered, suddenly concerned for the old man, and glanced toward the front door. "Do you think someone is trying to hurt Grover?"

He slowly shook his head. "I fear it's much worse than that."

He strode to the front door, and I hurried behind him. He knocked several times, and we waited. Just when I'd begun to lose hope that Grover would answer, Gideon met my gaze. "What did I teach you?"

I studied his beautiful blue eyes. "Patience."

He dipped his head. "That's right. We're letting him know that we have no intention of leaving."

I exhaled a cloud of stress, and he knocked again. This time with enough force that the door quivered on its hinges. It took Gideon two more times of doing the same, before I sensed a presence on the opposite side of the door. The lock clicked, and it slowly opened.

Grover glanced out. His eyes were so glazed that, for a moment, I thought he didn't recognize me. Bits of food clung to his unkempt beard, and he wore the same clothes that he had been in when I'd found him in the ice cream shop.

He glanced between Gideon and me. When he finally spoke, his voice was raspy. "Daisy."

My heart broke for the poor older man. Where he'd seemed okay before, guilt now rolled off him in waves. I placed a hand over my heart. "Oh, Grover. What have you done?"

He turned from us, leaving the door wide open, and shuffled into the living room. The stench of rotted food was everywhere, and Grover smelled awful himself. He sat in his rocker and stared at the TV that was on with the sound down.

Gideon and I moved to stand directly in front of him, and eventually, he lifted his gaze. This time, he focused on Gideon instead of me. "I expect you're here for me."

I jerked my gaze to Gideon, about to accuse him of keeping secrets, but I found confusion on his face as well.

He gave a small shake of his head. "No."

Grover blinked as though that would clear away his obvious bewilderment. "But you're a..."

Gideon shot me a sideways glance full of concern. "There's something wrong," he said in a low voice.

Tendrils of fear wrapped around me, making it hard to breathe. I had no idea what was happening, but I feared it was significant. "What is it?"

Instead of responding, he focused on Grover. "Did you or did you not take Merry Mercer's life?"

An anguished sob came from deep within his chest. "I did. I couldn't let Fern's legacy be tarnished by such a person."

I inhaled a breath full of despair. "Oh, Grover. Why? You know that the Goddess's choice is never wrong. If you'd just left things up to her, she'd have done her job perfectly. You have now killed a woman who was never going to end up in that council seat in the first place."

He met my gaze, his pale eyes full of tears. "I had to. I couldn't take the chance of someone tarnishing her legacy. She was too special for that."

The dear man was so confused. That couldn't be held against him, could it? "But why sell your soul, too?"

"I was afraid I couldn't accomplish it on my own. I haven't the strength." He paused to wipe his eyes. "To make a deal was the only way I could be sure."

Uncertainty triggered my anxiety, and I looked at Gideon. "So, he sold his soul to a demon to keep Merry off the council but that demon wasn't you?"

His eyes were full of the disquiet I felt. "No. Not me. In fact, no contract that would affect Merry should have been allowed to come to fruition at that time."

A small tremor began deep inside me. "What do we do?"

Instead of answering, he turned to Grover. "We will need to take you to the police station."

Grover seemed shocked and perplexed by Gideon's response. "The police? But I thought..."

Gideon released a heavy exhale. "I am not the one who contracted with you. Therefore, I am not the one who can collect."

Grover still seemed confused. "The police?" he asked again.

I stepped forward to help him up, but Gideon grabbed my arm, stopping me. "Permit me."

Things were at play that I didn't understand, but I did recognize Gideon's urge to protect me. I swallowed and took a step back.

Grover was hesitant to accept Gideon's outstretched hand, but he finally did. "I need to use the bathroom before we leave."

Gideon nodded and released his hand. Grover shuffled toward the hallway, looking more tired than I'd ever seen him. I lifted my gaze to Gideon, knowing my expression would be full of the fear that I felt in every inch of my body. "I don't understand what's happening."

He gave me a halfhearted smile and drew the side of his thumb down my cheek. "My dearest Daisy. Fear not. I will protect you."

His answer wasn't good enough. "From what though? What is going on?"

"I can't be sure at the moment. I need to talk to others first."

My mind wouldn't accept his response. I needed more. "Am I right that you made a deal with Merry but someone else made a deal with Grover? And that shouldn't have been able to happen because it interfered with your original contract?"

His smile grew bigger. "You are correct, Detective Daisy."

A loud thump came from down the hall, interrupting our conversation. Alarm colored Gideon's features as he glanced toward the sound and then back at me. "Go outside, Daisy."

I shook my head. "But—"

His eyes darkened to black. *"Now."*

I hurried from him and raced toward the front door. Once I was outside, I slammed it behind me and didn't stop until I was next to his Mercedes. I wanted to find sanctuary inside the car, but that was Gideon's domain, and I didn't know who to trust at the moment.

Instead, I stayed near the back bumper with my arms folded protectively in front of me and listened. I closed my eyes, trying as hard as I could to hear any kind of sound. But there was nothing but the chirping of birds in the trees and a dog barking in the distance.

It felt like an eternity had passed before Gideon emerged, but it was likely only minutes. He strode toward me, seeming composed, but I could sense that he wasn't. He reached me and rubbed his hands from my shoulders to my elbows several times. "Are you okay?"

I shook my head and then shrugged. "I don't know. I guess. What happened in there?"

He stared at me, and I felt him trying to connect on an emotional level. "Grover chose to end his life on his own. I'll spare you the gruesome details, but he ingested a poison that stopped his heart almost immediately."

Overwhelming sadness cloaked me, and I placed my fingers against my lips to contain the sob that threatened. I shook my head several times before I felt controlled enough to speak. "Oh, Gideon. How could he have done such a thing?"

He stared back and forth between my eyes and then without warning, pulled me against him and wrapped me in his embrace. He held me like that, and I didn't resist. I was grateful for the comfort he offered.

Then he kissed my hair and released me. "I cannot explain why people make the choices they do. But creating a contract was obviously something Grover strongly believed in, though it was an unnecessary sacrifice on his part. The worst is that he will not be reunited with his beloved Fern in the afterlife."

That was hard to accept. "But what if he wasn't in his right mind when he created the contract or when he stabbed Merry?"

Gideon shrugged. "These things are not mine to consider. I know nothing of what happens after a soul departs. But my impression is that the contracts are unbreakable."

I considered his words and then met his gaze. "What about his soul? Did the other...demon who created the contract arrive to accept it?"

He shook his head. "I cannot collect from another's contract unless the spirit leaves the body willingly, which of course, Grover's did once his became uninhabitable, so I collected for him. I could have allowed his spirit to linger until the owner of the contract arrived, but I chose not to do so even though it can complicate things."

"I see." Though I didn't really.

The sound of sirens echoed in the distance, and I widened my eyes in question.

He lifted his chin. "Yes, I called them. We will need to tell them everything we know, but please, if you would be so kind, keep my final interference out of it."

I nodded. "I'll keep your secret."

He looped an arm around my neck, tugging my head close, and he kissed my hair again.

EPILOGUE

The following morning, I stood in my mostly empty coffee shop, staring out the large window, and watched rain pour from the heavens. I couldn't help but feel Mother Earth was attempting to wash away the sins and tears from recent events in Sweet Mountain Meadows.

By now, the news of what Grover had done had circulated the town multiple times, and the moods of most everyone I'd seen that morning reflected it. Fern and Grover had both been beloved members of our community, and it was baffling to think how things could have gone so wrong.

It wasn't until late the previous night that I'd realized I had never gotten the chance to ask Grover why he'd picked my knife to murder Merry. Had he shuffled through everyone's things at one point and just picked the first athame he'd come across? When he'd gifted Fern's knife to me, had he known? Was he trying to compensate for using mine? Unless he'd journaled about it somewhere, I would never know.

One thing I was certain of was that I wouldn't be using Fern's ritual knife in the future, either. Hers and mine had both been tainted with too much negativity, more so than I believed could ever be cleansed or cast away with a spell.

I hadn't heard from Gideon after he'd dropped me off the previous day. We had both been too exhausted to spend much time talking about events, and I knew he had business of some sort to take care of. Obviously, the rules in his world hadn't been followed, but I didn't know exactly what that entailed. Perhaps he would explain it sometime.

That was if I saw him again.

Now that we'd discovered the murderer and Gideon was certain I wouldn't be charged, his business in Sweet Mountain Meadows had concluded. There was no reason for him to remain.

I couldn't picture him leaving town without saying goodbye, but I also didn't know if his job had required him to leave right away, either.

I sighed and turned away from the window and caught Aeri watching me from behind the counter. Luckily, after everything that had happened the previous day, no one questioned my despondent mood.

I gestured toward the Purry Parlor with a tilt of my head. "I'm going to hang out with Freya for a bit. I'll keep an eye out here, and if things get busy, I'll be right out."

She nodded but didn't speak.

Inside the parlor, I found Nicole sitting on the floor, brushing Old Grey. I could hear his purrs the second I stepped inside. "Someone's happy," I said.

Nicole smiled, but sadness hovered around her as well. "You know how he loves to be brushed."

I did indeed. "I'm going to hang out with you guys and Freya for a bit."

At the sound of her name, Freya left her perch high on the wall and jumped down several cascading shelves until she was even with my shoulders. I reached out and pulled her to my chest, kissing her head as I did. Which, unfortunately, reminded me of Gideon.

I sank into the chair where he'd once sat and lifted the footrest while reclining the back of the seat at the same time. Freya settled on my chest, and she regarded me with worried eyes.

"Hey," Nicole said. "If you're going to be in here for a bit, is it okay if I run a quick errand?"

I nodded without meeting her gaze. I'd rather be alone with my kitties anyway. "Sure."

She was gone only a minute when the door opened again. I turned to ask what she'd forgotten, but I found Gideon standing in the doorway instead. I quickly raised my seat into a sitting position and stood. He walked closer, and I headed toward him as well.

Though part of me wished I hadn't, because being close allowed me to see the sadness swimming in his eyes. "Hello, lovely Daisy."

"Hi," I managed and lowered Freya to the ground before I looked into his eyes once more. "Is everything okay?"

I didn't have to ask to know, but I did anyway.

He lifted a thumb and drew it down my cheek. "My dearest lovely Daisy. I've come to say goodbye."

The muscles in my throat gathered into a tight knot, and emotion churned deep within me. I used every bit of strength I had to keep it contained. "It's time, huh?"

He curved his lips into something that resembled a smile. "I will come back though."

I wouldn't ask him when because if he named a date and he didn't show then life would be unbearable for a while. Instead, I preferred to think of his return as sometime in the future. Something to look forward to.

It was my turn to force a smile. "Thank you for helping me clear my name."

The warmth reached his eyes this time. "Of course. Thank you for the loveliest time. I can't say that I've experienced anything quite like my time here."

I hoped that was a good thing. "Do you have to leave right now? Or do we have time for an early lunch?"

He shook his head. "I'm afraid I must go now."

I nodded and then stuck out my hand for him to shake.

He folded his fingers around mine, but instead of shaking my hand, he used his grip to tug me forward. He folded me into an embrace, and I couldn't resist placing my hands on his shoulders. "I will miss you," he whispered and lowered his mouth to mine.

His kiss was sweet and tender, and he ignited feelings inside me that I'd thought were long dead. When he released me and moved away, I felt as if he'd taken my breath and my heart with him.

He stared at me for a long moment, dipped his head, and then turned. I said nothing as he walked away, something I regretted the moment he was out of sight.

But there was no sense chasing after him and asking him to stay. He had to go. I knew that. But I would cling to the hope that he'd return much sooner than later.

Until then, I would take care of myself, my kitties, and my mom. I would try hard to prove to Jocelyn that she was right to put her faith in me.

And I would wait.

***

Book Two, For Once in My Midlife Coming October 2021.

Keep reading for an excerpt from Book One of the Teas and Temptations series titled Once Wicked. If you've already enjoyed that series, you can check out the Crystal Cove Cozy Mystery Series, where Gideon makes his first appearance.

Dear Reader:

Thanks for joining me on another journey inside Hazel's world. I hope you enjoyed the story. If you did, please consider leaving a review. It's simple, and it helps me in a profound way to continue to bring you stories you enjoy. All you need to do is:

Return to the purchasing page.

Scroll down to the <u>Customer Review Section</u>.

Look for <u>Review This Product</u>

Click on <u>Write A Customer Review</u>

Your review helps me tremendously, and it can be as simple as a short and sweet, "I liked it".

Also, make sure to sign up for my newsletter and follow me on Amazon for release news of future books and for special offers.

Newsletter signup: www.CindyStark.com

Amazon: https://www.amazon.com/Cindy-Stark/e/B008FT394W

Thank you, very much, and happy reading,
Cindy

Excerpt from Once Wicked
Teas and Temptations Cozy Mysteries
Book One

Hazel Hardy's thighs burned as she pedaled her bicycle up the incline toward the big Victorian manor at the top of the hill.

She'd pulled her auburn hair into a ponytail to keep the loose curls out of her face while she rode. Between jeans and her favorite olive-green sweater, along with the exercise, she'd stay warm enough.

It was only mid-March, and the days could still carry a chill. Luckily, this year, they'd been blessed with unseasonably warm weather and the sun was out today, bright and warm, so she'd be just fine.

She'd tucked tins of her handcrafted teas in the bike's basket, and they bumped against each other with each pedal, clanging out a metallic tune. She couldn't picture a more beautiful small town than Stonebridge, Massachusetts, with its tree-lined streets coursing between a mixture of newer buildings and centuries-old rock-hewn churches. For an earth witch, it was perfect.

No matter where Hazel went, she always found a smiling face. Her mom had missed the mark completely when she'd warned her a few months back about the town that still harbored hatred against witches going on three hundred years.

But Hazel had yearned to learn more about her heritage, and the people she'd met in Stonebridge were as nice as sweetened chamomile tea at bedtime. The cherry on top was that she'd never have to see Victor's cheating face again.

Filling her lungs repeatedly to compensate for her thumping heart, she gave a last burst of energy to wheel up the Winthrop's driveway. Hopefully all this biking would compensate for her obsession with cherry macaroons and hazelnut cannoli.

A loud horn battered her eardrums from behind, sending her into a panic. She turned the handlebars to the right in a quick, knee-jerk reaction to avoid the threat. Her front tire slid sideways as she struggled to keep her bike upright. She wobbled to the left and teetered to the right.

When her front tire hit soft gravel off the edge of the driveway, her bike launched her like an angry bull did a novice cowboy.

The palms of her hands took the brunt of the landing. She skidded for a moment before rolling to a stop.

Unladylike curses hovered on her tongue, and she swiveled her head, ready to unleash her rage.

Overweight, gray-haired, and full of himself, Winston Winthrop didn't spare her a glance as he drove his black Mercedes past her and parked between the sparkling fountain and elegant house.

Hazel struggled to catch a decent breath as she got to her feet. She wiped her dusty, scraped up palms on her jeans.

Across the drive, Winthrop's manservant dashed from the house to open his employer's car door.

Up until this point, Hazel hadn't come face-to-face with her client's husband. But she was about to now. She'd heard rumors of the self-important, rude man, but she'd had a hard time believing such a man could be married to the sweet and gentle Mrs. Winthrop.

Apparently, she'd been wrong.

Hazel hobbled to where her bike had fallen after her spectacular dismount, and she lifted it from the ground, inspecting it for damage. Lucky for Mr. Winthrop, her favorite mode of transportation remained intact. She picked up the tin boxes of tea and placed them in the basket, grateful they'd survived as well.

She strode toward the house, walking as fast as her tender knees would allow.

As she approached, the wealthy aristocrat dropped his keys into the hands of his employee. "Do take care to keep the drive clear, Mick. We wouldn't want anyone to get hurt."

Hazel opened her mouth to give Mr. Winthrop the verbal lashing he deserved, but Mick shook his head in warning, a lock of the twenty-something man's dark hair falling into his eyes.

Mr. Winthrop walked toward the house, exuding a privileged air. "And do get yourself a haircut," he called over his shoulder. "We've had enough trouble with witches and beggars in the past. I can't continue to employ anyone looking so unkempt."

Hazel clenched her jaw. "*Witches and beggars?*" She spat out the offensive words to Mick. If she could make one wish, she'd hope never to encounter the nasty man again.

She'd never tell her mother she'd been right about the residents of Stonebridge who still believed those who practiced witchcraft were spawns of Satan, a notion some residents had passed down for generations, since the early colonization of the area. Up until this moment, she hadn't witnessed evidence of such despicable and unfounded attitudes toward others, and even now, her heart didn't want to believe it was true.

Witches were not the devil's disciples, and she took issue with anyone who thought they were. Honoring Mother Earth and her gifts was anything but evil.

If there was a rotten egg in the bunch, it was Mr. Winthrop.

Mick cast a wary glance toward the house and then switched his dark gaze back to Hazel. "Ignore him. He's an old man out of touch with reality."

She liked Mick Ramsey, though she couldn't get a clear reading from his soul. He had many emotional walls, though that alone didn't make him bad. Sometimes people erected barriers to hide something. Other times, their walls were for protection.

She liked to think it was the latter, and he just needed a friend.

Hazel snorted. "I'd like to show him reality."

"Wouldn't we all?" Mick countered.

She considered her options. A healthy dose of the itches...in a very uncomfortable place? A potion that would leave his stomach heaving? The thought of Mr. Winthrop trying discreetly to take care of his issues brought a smile back to her face.

Mick nodded to the white woven basket on the front of her pink bike. "Tea for Mrs. Winthrop?"

She smiled, grateful to focus on something else. "Every Monday. Speaking of which, I'd better hurry. I'm already behind, and the matron of the kitchen, as I like to call her, gets snippy when she has to wait for me."

He laughed and shook his head. "That's one woman I try to avoid at all costs."

"Mrs. Jones isn't that bad," Hazel said, and they both laughed because they knew she was. "Catch you later."

She parked her bicycle alongside the garage and retrieved one of several tins from the woven basket. With her delivery safe in her tenderized hands, she followed the flat stone path around the side of the elaborate home to the back door where she didn't bother to knock.

"Hello?" she called as she entered, and immediately Mrs. Jones, the curmudgeonly cook appeared from inside the pantry.

"Good morning, Hazel." Mrs. Jones graced her with a never-before-seen smile that surprised her.

She took a few seconds to recover from the shock. "Good morning to you, too. You seem particularly happy today." Perhaps she'd misjudged her. After all, working for Mr. Winthrop could make anyone ornery.

Mrs. Jones widened her eyes as though also surprised, and the bright aura hovering around her dimmed. "Nonsense. I'm no happier than any other day."

Hazel stared at her for a long moment, sad that the woman had chosen to return to unhappiness. She sighed and held up the tin. "I have Mrs. Winthrop's tea delivery."

Mrs. Jones jerked her head toward the stove. "Her tea service is ready to go. Just waiting on you. I've been keeping the water hot for the past fifteen minutes."

And, just like that, the waspish old woman was back. "Sorry. I stopped at June Porter's first, and she can...well, you know..." How did she say this without being rude? "She likes her conversation."

The cook grunted. "Best keep your hands on your ears when she's around, or she'll talk them off before she sends you on your way."

Hazel smiled in agreement and headed toward the tea service Mrs. Jones had prepared. She could have mentioned her unfortunate incident outside, but she doubted she'd gain any sympathy. "I'll just wash my hands and head on up."

She hesitated for a moment, reluctant to ask her question. "Shall I put away the remaining tea?"

Mrs. Jones lifted a sarcastic brow. "Does anyone touch anything in my kitchen? Ever?"

"No." Hazel answered, the same as she had the other four weeks she'd been delivering tea. It seemed wrong to leave it for Mrs. Jones, but the woman barely tolerated Hazel as it was. Hazel quickly finished her task and headed for the elaborate staircase with the mahogany handrail and turned balusters that she loved so much.

The home Hazel had rented was older as well and had retained an air of history with arched doorways and decorative moulding between the ceiling and walls. But where her house was akin to a common person, Mrs. Winthrop's was the grand lady of the town, and Hazel never tired of visiting.

When Hazel's new assistant at her shop, Hazel's Teas and Temptations, had suggested door-to-door service to increase her customer base and therefore revenue, Hazel had questioned her sanity. People wanted pizza delivered, not tea.

But Gretta had been right to an extent. Many of the fifty and older crowd of ladies of Stonebridge loved the idea of gourmet tea being delivered straight to their doors, especially when they learned Mrs. Winthrop had signed up for the service. Most of these women came from prominent families who had lived in Massachusetts since colonial times, and they had the money to show for it.

Mrs. Winthrop's influence had sent Hazel's bottom line sailing into the black, and she couldn't be more grateful.

Which was why she'd agreed to also serve a pot of her gourmet tea every Monday to Mrs. Winthrop, allowing time for lovely conversation with a woman who rarely left her house. It was the least Hazel could do to show her gratitude, and besides, she'd found she enjoyed their time together, too.

The stairs of the old house creaked as Hazel ascended, a sentry of sorts, announcing her arrival. Hazel followed the now-familiar path she always took to the end of the hall and then knocked on the last door on the left.

"Come in," Mrs. Winthrop said.

Hazel balanced the tray on one hand and turned the doorknob.

Inside, sixty-nine-year-old Florence Winthrop sat at a Victorian dressing table with several bottles of nail polish in front of her. Patterned gold on ivory walls were the backdrop for the elegantly carved mahogany bed that dominated the room, complete with a gorgeous dusty rose quilt that matched the color of the curtains.

"Good morning, Mrs. Winthrop." Hazel made her way to the small table and two chairs near the window where they always drank tea. She lowered the tray that also carried some delicious-looking blueberry scones and Florence's joint supplements to the table and turned back to her client.

The frail woman graced her with a smile. "Good morning to you, my dear, and, please, call me Florence. We've known each other long enough, and calling me Mrs. Winthrop makes me feel old."

"Of course." Hazel gave her an approving nod. "I'm glad to see you're up and out of bed early this morning."

Some days, Mrs. Winthrop, make that Florence, had still been asleep when she'd arrived. Her ailments, whatever they were, tired the poor woman something fierce and added a good ten years to her looks though she really wasn't that old at all.

Florence graced her with a smile. "Today is a good day. Hardly any pain at all."

"I'm so happy to hear that." Hazel found it difficult not to add a little something to her tea to help with those aches and pains, but she'd promised her mother she'd not use any potions or spells whilst in Stonebridge.

The whole idea that she'd had to promise to her mother seemed silly, but the town had a history of murdering innocent witches. Long ago, her ancestors had run in the middle of the night to escape persecution.

Times had changed, but, apparently not as much as she would have expected.

Hazel moved to the dressing table and inspected the array of nail polish. "Looks like you're planning to get dressed up. Is Mr. Winthrop taking you out on the town?"

Florence snorted and shook her head. "No, nothing special. Albert and I haven't dated in years." She shrugged. "I just wanted to do something small to feel pretty."

She met Hazel's gaze with a sad one of her own. "I haven't felt pretty in so long. If only I could be young again like you and Rachel."

Hazel gave her a kind smile. "You're a very beautiful woman, Florence. Rachel and I don't have anything on you."

Though Hazel also envied the Winthrop maid's figure. She wouldn't mind having her sleek blond hair, too, as opposed to her own unruly auburn curls that tended to get out of hand at times.

Mrs. Winthrop stood and placed a hand on the dressing table to steady herself. "You have your youth, and that's what men want. That's what we all want."

She linked her arm through Mrs. Winthrop's and led her to the tea table.

"Be a dear and bring the polish, too, won't you? Perhaps you can help me paint my nails after we've had tea."

Hazel returned and scooped up the six different bottles of polish. One by one, she set them along the side of the tea table before she took her seat. Her so-called tea delivery service had become more of a social service, but she didn't mind. The ladies in town who chose that service appreciated the company and didn't mind paying extra for Hazel's time.

Plus, as her assistant, Gretta, suggested, it was a great way to get to know the town's residents and ingratiate herself with them.

"I brought a new flavor today," Hazel said as she set a tea strainer in Florence's cup. "It's a strawberry green tea blend."

The older woman lifted the teacup and held it near her nose. "That smells divine, Hazel. Do I detect traces of grapefruit in there?"

"Nose of a bloodhound," she said with a smile. "No one could get anything past you."

Florence winked and touched the tip of her nose. "Not to say that they haven't tried."

"A fool's errand," she said, and they both chuckled.

Hazel poured hot water into both of their cups and picked up a bottle of light pink polish while the tea leaves steeped. "This is a lovely color. May I?"

"Certainly. We should both paint our nails before you leave."

Hazel opened the bottle and drew the brush across one of her nails, leaving a lovely shade of pink in its path. "So pretty."

Florence agreed.

After they'd finished their tea and blueberry scones that Mrs. Jones had provided for them, Florence lifted a bottle of cherry red polish. "I think I should like this color."

Hazel let out a low whistle and grinned. "Perfect for a sexy siren like yourself."

Florence blushed bright pink. "Stop, young lady. You'll embarrass me."

"All right." Hazel didn't want to tease her too much. "Give me your hand."

The older woman spread a napkin over the gleaming wooden table and laid her hand out, palm down. With careful, precise strokes, Hazel painted bright red on each of the woman's nails.

When she finished, she set back with a smile. "Gorgeous."

A smile crept across Florence's face. "I used to wear this shade all the time when I was younger, back before this damned disease crippled me."

Hazel yearned to tell her how sorry she was that she'd been afflicted as she had, but that would help nothing. "Any time you want me to paint them, just ask." She lifted a bottle of clear polish. "How about a top coat so your color will last longer?"

The woman rolled her eyes and shook her head. "Not that one. It works a little too well."

Hazel laughed. "How can it work too well?"

"It stays on even after you want it to come off. I don't want red nails forever." She pushed the clear coat aside. "Use the other one."

"I understand completely. I once had a beautiful shade of gold polish with flecks of glitter in it. I used tons of cotton balls soaked with polish remover before I could get it off. Such a pain."

"Exactly." The older woman agreed with a firm nod of her head.

Hazel selected a second bottle of top coat and applied it to the woman's nails. "There. You look like you've just come from the beauty salon."

She beamed as she examined her hands. "I do. Wait until Albert sees. Now, finish your nails before you need to leave."

"Yes—"

A terrified scream for help cut her short. Her gaze flew to Florence's. "Someone's hurt."

Color drained from the older woman's face as Hazel jumped to her feet. "Good Lord. Go. Please," she commanded.

Hazel dashed into the hall. She followed the sounds of commotion to the opposite end of the floor and entered a bedroom where several people had gathered including Mick and Mrs. Jones.

Mr. Winthrop lay sprawled on the bed. His eyes bulged from their sockets as though he, too, was stunned.

Their young maid with sleek blond hair sat on the floor near his bed, her nakedness only partially covered by an ivory throw. She'd buried her face against the mattress, but Hazel could see from her shaking shoulders that she sobbed.

Hazel's heart lurched in sickening thumps, and she glanced at the stoic faces around her. *"Why is no one doing anything?"* She stepped forward.

Mick gripped her arm, stopping her. He shook his head. "It's too late. He's dead."

Hazel jerked her arm free. "How do you know? If it's a heart attack, maybe he can be revived."

Rachel sobbed harder. "I wanted to help." Her words came out between frantic breaths. "But he was frothing at the mouth and convulsing..." She stilled, her dark eyes wet and rimmed with red. "Like a rabid dog," she whispered.

Hazel did take a step back then. She couldn't imagine what kind of disease or disorder would make a person froth at the mouth, but it couldn't be good.

"What is it?" A feeble voice came from behind them. "What's happened?"

Hazel cringed. Mrs. Winthrop. She couldn't see this. Not her dead husband that she'd wanted to impress only moments before. Not the naked woman who'd obviously been with him doing things they shouldn't when he'd died.

No wife should ever witness something like this.

Hazel turned from the gathered crowd and met Florence in the hall. She took the woman's chilly hands in hers. "I'm so sorry, Florence." She would hide it all from her if she could. "It's your husband."

"Albert?" She shot a frantic gaze beyond Hazel's shoulder. "What's wrong?"

Hazel closed her eyes for a long moment, not wanting to be the one to deliver the news. Then she met the new widow's gaze. "He's dead."

Florence screamed and collapsed against Hazel.

"Help, please," Hazel cried out.

Mick emerged into the hall and gathered Florence into his arms. "Let's get her to bed, and you can stay with her while I call the police."

BOOK LIST

SWEET MOUNTAIN WITCHES (PG-Rated Fun):
Midlife or Death
For Once in My Midlife

CRYSTAL COVE COZY MYSTERIES (PG-Rated Fun):
Murder and Moonstones
Brews and Bloodstone
Curses and Carnelian
Killer Kyanite
Rumors and Rose Quartz
Hexes and Hematite

TEAS & TEMPTATIONS COZY MYSTERIES (PG-Rated Fun):
Once Wicked
Twice Hexed
Three Times Charmed
Four Warned
The Fifth Curse
It's All Sixes
Spellbound Seven
Elemental Eight
Nefarious Nine
Hijacked Honeymoon
A Witch Without a Spell

BLACKWATER CANYON RANCH (Western Sexy Romance):
Caleb
Oliver
Justin
Piper

Jesse

ASPEN SERIES (Small Town Sexy Romance):
Wounded (Prequel)
Relentless
Lawless
Cowboys and Angels
Come Back To Me
Surrender
Reckless
Tempted
Crazy One More Time
I'm With You
Breathless

PINECONE VALLEY (Small Town Sexy Romance):
Love Me Again
Love Me Always

RETRIBUTION NOVELS (Sexy Romantic Suspense):
Branded
Hunted
Banished
Hijacked
Betrayed

ARGENT SPRINGS (Small Town Sexy Romance):
Whispers
Secrets

OTHER TITLES:
Moonlight and Margaritas
Sweet Vengeance

ABOUT THE AUTHOR

Award-winning author Cindy Stark lives in a small town shadowed by the Rocky Mountains. She enjoys creating magical mayhem in her witch cozy mysteries, unexpected twists in her emotional romantic suspense, and forever love with hot guys in her sexy contemporary romance stories.

She'd like to think she's the boss of her three adorable and sassy cats, but deep down, she knows she's ruled by kitty overlords. Someday, she hopes to earn enough to open a cat sanctuary where she can save all the kitties and play all day with toe beans and murder mittens.

Connect with her online at:
http://www.CindyStark.com
http://facebook.com/CindyStark19
https://www.amazon.com/Cindy-Stark/e/B008FT394W

Made in United States
Orlando, FL
08 March 2022